THE RED ROCK KILLER

DELUXE EDITION

EDAN SZE MYSTERY
BOOK ONE

MELISSA YI

Dedicated to my mother and the International Thriller Writers

Join Melissa's mailing list at www.melissayuaninnes.com or Kickstart her at https://www.kickstarter.com/profile/ melissayi

Copyright © 2024 by Melissa Yuan-Innes

Published by Olo Books & Windtree Press

Cover design © 2024 by The Cover Collection

Yi, Melissa, author   The Red Rock Killer / Melissa Yi. (Edan Sze mystery novel; 1)
Issued in print and electronic formats.
ISBN 978-1-998758-16-6 (hardcover).--ISBN 978-1-998758-14-2 (softcover deluxe).—
ISBN 978-1-998758-17-3 (epub deluxe)   I. Title.   C813'.6

Although no children are harmed directly, this novel includes references to death and gunfire. Please feel free to skip to chapter 48 if needed.

To advise of typographical errors, please contact <u>olobooks@gmail.com</u>

Las Vegas
RED ROCK
CANYON
N.C.A.
159
215
8
37
mp MTS
Charleston Pk.
11,918
Enjoy!

1

My mom told me I could do whatever I wanted the whole summer I turned fourteen, so I decided to find the Red Rock Killer.[1]

Let me back up. I sure hadn't expected to find death the morning that me and my two best friends hiked the Red Rock Canyon[2], a conservation area 15 miles west of Las Vegas.

That Saturday morning, Callie Yang woke up me and Barstow right after rolling up her sleeping bag. "Let's do Red Rock! Please."

"No thanks, Cal. I downloaded a new game on Steam, and Edan wants to play Terraria." Barstow Ness glanced at me for support while he hooked his glasses back behind his ears.

Now, I am NOT a hiker. I read, I game, I dance/flail with 1 Million Dance Studio's online tutorials, and I research the Civil War for fun. In other words, I run *away* from fresh air and trees.[3]

"'We need the tonic of wildness,'" said Callie, wrapping her silky black hair in a bun. She's a swimmer and likes running 5K's for fun and crap like that.

I gave her the side eye, even though it's hard to get mad at her when she looks like a ballerina with more shoulder muscles. "Is that a Mr. Carver quote?" Our history teacher writes a quote on the blackboard every day, using real chalk. He's old school.

"No. I read it myself. It's Henry David Thoreau."

Barstow and I both raised our eyebrows at her.

"Okay, I read it on Goodreads. So what? It's still true. I hate being cooped up in school all week and then gaming with you two all weekend. It's my *birthday* in nine days. I need to get out with my Garden of Eden and my Barstonia."

I groaned. My name is Edan Sze[4]. Edan is Celtic for fire, which Mom says is perfect for a baby born in the desert.

It's pronounced Ed<u>e</u>n, as in the Garden of. Since Sze sounds a bit like the letter Z, a few kids call me E-Z. Whatever works.

Callie had invoked the birthday rule. The birthday girl or boy gets to choose what we do on the big day. So we all got suited up for Red Rock, which meant sunscreen, socks, and running shoes. Everyone filled up their water bottles, officially ending the sleepover at my place.

I don't know why, but my friends love coming over to our second floor apartment, even though the place is so small that I sleep on the living room couch and they have to push the coffee table toward the kitchen to make room for their sleeping bags on the floor. Not to mention that our downstairs neighbour, Mr. Villalobos, bangs on his ceiling with a broom handle if we walk too loud.

Mr. Villalobos also mixes up me and Callie because we're both Asian girls, even though I'm shorter, plumper, and dyed the tips of my hair red. At least he can tell the difference between us and Barstow, a slim Black dude.

"Can your mom give us a ride?" asked Callie.

I yawned and checked my watch. Only 7 a.m. on a Sunday in June. Callie wakes up freakishly early because she hits the pool about now, and Barstow has insomnia. I'm the only kid who likes to sleep in like a normal person.

"Is *he* here?" Barstow whispered. He didn't mean Mr. Villalobos.

I took a few steps into the front hallway and paused in front of the bathroom doorway to stare at the white solid wood door to Mom's room. She'd gone on a date with her police boyfriend, Garrett Smith, last night. The closed door meant that she or both of them had come back while we crashed.

Barstow avoids the police, and I don't blame him. His parents are successful entrepreneurs who run the Parent Teacher Association, but that won't protect Barstow from a bullet. #BlackLivesMatter.

"We could take Wheelzz to Lovell Canyon," said Callie, naming a local ride share.

"It's your birthday. I'll get it," said Barstow, already opening the Wheelzz app on his phone. His generous parents had set up a family account so he could book himself rides.

I shot him a grateful look. Mom doesn't make tons of cash as a secretary for the Las Vegas Police Department. The Red Rock Canyon is a whole half hour's drive away, depending on traffic. "My present will be your visitor fee," I told Callie, checking my change purse. I touched the emergency $20 folded in my front right pocket, but that's emergency money, like in case I get mugged.

Callie grinned. "We get in free 'cause we're under 16."

"Yay! I'll chip in for the ride," I told Barstow.

"E-Z, your money no good here,"[5] Barstow said, standing up.

"They'll be here in twelve." Just enough time to roll up my sheets and his sleeping bag, shove everything behind the couch, and slide the coffee table back in place in case Garrett woke up and threw a fit over the mess.

We grabbed apples and our water bottles and tiptoed past Mr. Villalobos's apartment on ground level, but our neighbor followed us to the front door and shook his withered fist at us anyway. "You woke me up again. You sound like elephants."

"Sorry, Mr. Villalobos." Callie awarded him her best smile. She gets along the best with grown-ups.

"Were you moving furniture? I'll call the cops next time for noise pollution."

"Sorry, Mr. Villalobos," Barstow and I called before slipping into our Wheelzz, a black Buick.

The driver, a middle-aged white guy in a button down shirt, listened to talk radio instead of chatting. Fine by us. He dropped us off in front of a sign that asked us to brush our shoes off to prevent the spread of invasive weeds. I did, even though only sand fell back out of my sneaker treads. "I never thought that we'd bring invasive species here," I said.

"Edan, *human beings* are an invasive species," said Barstow.

Callie gave him a high five before holding up her other hand for me.

I tapped it and tried to look cool while I segued into a quote I'd memorized. "'It looks to me as though some men try to see how depraved they can be. Gambling, Card Playing, Profanity, Sabbath Breaking—'"

"What are you talking about?" Callie wrinkled her forehead.

"A quote from the Civil War. Between battles, the soldiers distracted themselves with gambling and swearing and other stuff. I figure it's a trauma response. For my history project, I'll divide the class into Blue and Grey. Mr. Carver said we could bet toothpicks on who'd win—"

"ANYway," Callie cut me off, "thanks for hiking. I know you don't like to move."

"Rude," said Barstow, while I protested, "I like to move my eyeballs for reading and video games."

"Moves your fingers too," said Barstow.

"Totally." Our turn for a high five.

"Just sayin', it's extra special that you came out for my birthday," said Callie.

I smiled at her. She's one of my favorite people in the world, even though I don't usually tell her. "HBD, Yang."

At barely 7:40 a.m., on a relatively remote trail, I saw zero other people. Comforting yet also creepy. I texted my mom a pic of the three of us at the trailhead with a backdrop of a bunch of trees, partly for geolocation.

"Those are pinyon or juniper trees, I think," said Callie.

Barstow grunted. He's bigger than both of us and arguably likes inertia more than I do, but both of us amped up our best behavior for Callie's birthday favor.

I closed my eyes to smell the trees, which smelled kind of like cedar and almost lemony. I wouldn't admit it to Callie yet, but I loved getting away from the traffic and the tourists. I could feel myself taking deeper breaths while my shoulders relaxed.

Callie and Barstow moved ahead of me. I admired our shoes making treads in the sandy trail, but my backpack plastered against my back with sweat. I lifted the straps away from my shoulders.

Partly as an excuse to slow down, I pointed at a sign for the Handy Peak Loop trail. "You want to go there? Sounds like good juju for your birthday."

"No!" Callie whipped off her sunglasses. "That's not a real trail. Stay on this path."

"Why is there a sign, then?" I carefully laid my backpack on my feet while I rested, letting my T-shirt air out.

"They're building it. It's not ready yet."

Barstow pulled out his phone. "We could check out the *beginning* of the Handy Peak Loop. They started to build it." He set off ahead of me, his shoes crunching in the sand.

I re-shouldered my backpack and followed him.

Callie hurried after us. "Hey. I'm the hiker." *And the athlete,* she didn't say. "If one of you breaks an ankle, it's me who has to get you out."

Barstow showed her the map on his cell phone.

She shook her head. "Not everywhere has reception. We're out of town."

Barstow twisted his phone to check the screen himself. "I've got three bars."

"You could lose them any time. Seriously."

"Even Barstow and me aren't getting lost by taking two steps," I said. Still, I started to turn around for the birthday girl, until I noticed something dark far in the distance, between the trees.

Something wider than a human, standing straight up, and unmoving.

"Don't go off-path," Callie shouted.

"I'm not moving, but you see that?" I pointed.

"Yes, sure. It looks like a barrel." Callie shrugged, while I squinted to focus on that black shape, a bit narrower at the top and bottom.

Yep, a barrel as tall as my chest, maybe 50 feet away. Barstow and I exchanged a look.

"What's a barrel doing here?" I asked.

"Maybe they're using it for construction?" Callie pointed back at the regular trail. Hint, hint.

"Everything's labeled for construction," said Barstow, shading his eyes and trying to make out a label. "You have to know what's inside. And they don't really use barrels, as far as I know."

"Maybe it's a rain barrel, like I asked for my birthday," I said. We need to collect rain whenever we can. Water is precious in the desert. I could do my part as long as Mr. Villalobos and other residents didn't freak out about unsightly barrels on our property.

Barstow shook his head. "You see a spigot? I sure don't."

"That barrel's in the trees and off-trail. C'mon, guys, let's go!" Callie's voice cracked.

I touched her shoulder. She pressed her lips together.

"Look." Barstow grimaced. "I know these National Parks. They don't clutter the landscape with garbage cans and rain barrels. My parents dragged me out to the main trails a few times. They keep rain barrels at the entrance, clearly labeled. Everything's a teaching opportunity, right? Those barrels were painted bright white with a green and blue raindrop. Not black and hidden in the trees."

My stomach curled in on itself.

"What are you saying?" Callie sweated under her sunscreen.

"I'm saying that we should take a picture of it and mark the spot. Then someone should call the park service and report the barrel. Just in case."

And that was how we first got mixed up with the Red Rock Killer.

2

M y phone rang Monday morning as I grabbed my history book out of my pale yellow locker.

"E-dawn Zee?"[1] said a woman's voice.

"No, *Eee*-d'n," I sighed, "as in the Garden of Eden."

"Please hold."

I stared at my phone. Why would someone call me and ask me to hold? Was this spam or worse? I only had five minutes before morning announcements.

"Hello, Edan." A different woman with a low, pleasant voice took over the call. "This is Officer Heather Peters. I want to talk to you about the barrel you and your friends found on Saturday. Could you come down to the station on South M.L.K.[2] Boulevard? It's the closest to your school."

I couldn't control my lips for a second. My mom worked in that station.

But I was the one who took the picture, called park services, and marked a line to the barrel on the sandy trail with my sneaker on Saturday. I couldn't deny it now.

"Edan? Can you hear me?"

"Yes, I can hear you," I whispered. I needed to text my friends, but not at the same time as talking to the police, in case I dropped the call on Officer Heather Peters.

Kids swarmed around me, talking and banging their lockers closed. One guy smelled like weed. I closed my eyes.

"Who are your friends?" Officer Peters continued. "In your message to Park Services, you said it was you and your friends."

"Um, I don't know," I said, willing myself not to say Barstow's name.

"Edan, I think you do know. I want you and your friends to come to the station as soon as you can."

"I'm in school," I said. Our principal, Mrs. Linkletter, would say, "Good morning, Foresters," any second now. She'd read the morning announcements and add something like, "Now remember, Foresters, save the planet and never gamble!" (Can you tell we live in Vegas? Teenagers can't gamble, although I hear casinos give out free snacks.[3])

"Yes, I know that," said the officer. "You go to Forester Middle School, right?"

"Right. And I'm not allowed to have my cell phone during class. I have to go. Sorry."

"Your classes end at 3 p.m. I expect you at the station with your friends by 4 at the latest. Is that clear, Edan?"

"Yes, ma'am. Goodbye now. I really have to go. Thank you."

I don't know where the thank you came from—I guess my mom drilled it into me—but Officer Peters said, "You're welcome. See you and your friends by 4, Edan," right before I shut off my phone and locked it in my locker.

At least she pronounced it. Eeeden. I barely managed to plunk my butt in the plastic seat before announcements started.

Callie gave me a strange look from the desk on my left. *You okay?* she mouthed.

I shook my head.

Barstow twisted around to frown from the desk in front of me, but he didn't say anything.

"Good morning, Foresters," said a man's voice. He didn't sound like Mrs. Linkletter.

We all looked confused, including our teacher, Mr. Carver, who sat at his desk under today's saying: *"History is always written wrong, and so always needs to be rewritten." George Santayana.*

Mr. Carver's big red mustache and beard usually disguised what he thought, except today his eyebrows went up and his beard drooped, kind of a cartoon version of surprise, while the announcements continued.

"This is your vice principal, Mr. Eisen. Your principal, Mrs. Linkletter, is away today. I'll let Sylvie Morgan take over in a moment, but I wanted to let all the Foresters know to stay on school property until 3 p.m. No one is allowed to leave our grounds during breaks or spare periods. I'll have more announcements soon, but today, that's all you need to know. Stay on school property. Check your emails for more details."

Did Mr. Eisen sound stressed? He's normally a cheerful bald guy who encourages us to sing Hanukkah songs during the winter holidays.

Barstow rummaged through his desk, stacking his books and restacking them, scowling furiously.

I chewed on the inside of my bottom lip, ignoring Callie's eyes boring into my left cheek.

3

All day, I wondered if I should call Officer Heather Peters. *Hi, we're locked in school, can't come.*

"Good excuse," said Barstow. "Don't go."

"I kind of have to go, though, right?"

"Right," said Callie, twirling her ponytail almost as much as she twisted her face. "I'm going with you. My parents said I should."

I held my palm up. She barely touched it in a weak high five, not like her at all.

"Sorry," said Barstow. He wouldn't look at us, and I knew he wouldn't talk to the police voluntarily. Time for me to take the pressure off.

"All good," I said, trying to smile. "Three's a crowd, right?"

Before the last bell rang, Mr. Eisen's voice crackled over the P.A. system. "Attention, Foresters. School has ended. You are to go home immediately. Do not deviate from your transportation home. Make sure to scan your pass on the bus, and we'll see you in the morning."

"Go home immediately," repeated Barstow, shouldering his backpack and slamming his locker door closed.

"My dad said he'd meet me at the police station," said Callie. "It's not home, but it's pretty safe, right?"

Barstow shook his head. "Good luck." He disappeared into the wave of kids heading for the buses, everyone quieter than usual.

"I think we'll be okay," I told Callie, pocketing my phone without checking it.

Callie and I hurried down to West Charleston Blvd and took the 206 to the enormous police station, a five-story stone and glass building that I'd never gone inside. We had to ring to enter, stand in the narrow, white doorway, and talk to a woman in uniform behind a counter on the right to tell her who we were and why we'd come.

The door directly facing the entrance, shut and combination-locked, finally swung open.[1]

Officer Peters walked us to a small conference room on the left, with two chairs and no table. "There's no need to be nervous. I'll ask you a few questions. The camera will be on at all times to record what you say. Does that sound good?"

I glanced at Callie. Her lips quivered, but she nodded, and I did too.

Officer Peters smiled at Callie before indicating a Black police officer with a shaved head and a small beard who stood in the doorway. "This is Mark Evans. He'll take you to your parents now."

I took a step forward, but Officer Peters held out her hand. "Edan, you'll stay with me."

They were separating us? Even as I opened my mouth to object, Callie followed Officer Evans, only glancing back at me once with wide eyes.

Before I could take a seat in the conference room, my mother rushed toward the other chair, her purse banging on her hip and her hands already reaching for me. "Edan. What's going on?"

Officer Peters said, "I'm glad you could make it, Ms. Sze.[2] Edan, tell me about Saturday morning."

At least she could pronounce my names now. I shifted in the hard plastic seat and tried to explain as best I could, leaving Barstow out of it. Callie loved to hike, and w—well, I'd—led them off-path. We found this barrel and decided to report it.

"What made you think the barrel was worth reporting?" Officer Peters asked.

Mom shook her head, and I tried to find the words. "Well, it was sort of strange to find it on this closed trail. Bar—um, barring any new design, we thought it didn't look like a rain barrel." I stopped. "Why, what was inside?"

The officer's expression didn't change. "We'll be making a press announcement shortly. I'm more interested in your reaction."

After pressing me for what felt like two hours, but turned out to be 45 minutes, Officer Peters finally ended with, "Thank you for your time, Edan."

I was sweating. I couldn't wait to compare notes with Callie. When Officer Peters opened the interview room door, though, Mom guided me through the hallway, outside the locked doors, and into the sunshine, while Callie left my texts unread.

"I'm fine," I insisted.

Later that night, though, I had to run and hug my old teddy bear when the police announced that they'd found a body inside the barrel.

4

EDAN

Did you hear? Body at Red Rock!

CALLIE

can't talk

I avoided my mother's eyes across our dining room table.

Mom's ballpoint pen scratched across the page of her small, pink diary before she asked for the tenth time, "Are you okay?"

"Sort of." I hadn't seen Callie since she'd split off with Officer Evans at the police station. Maybe she was in serious trouble. And I didn't want to bring up Barstow, since he supposedly hadn't come to Red Rock.

Mom closed her diary and tucked it on our bookshelf above the kitchen doorway before she clinked two mugs of green tea onto our rickety wooden table. "Edan."

"Yeah?" I shoved my phone in my pocket so she wouldn't catch any of our messages. The tea tasted a bit like honey, but I couldn't relax. "Is Garrett coming?"

She shook her head. "He's working overtime."

Phew. The last thing I needed was Officer Garrett Smith looming over me, asking what we were doing at Red Rock.

At the police press conference, they'd announced that a woman's body was found 15 miles west of Las Vegas. My finger trembled when I checked that yep, that was Red Rock.

A body. A woman's body.

They wanted to identify her and contact family members before they made any further announcements.

I warmed my hands on my mug and asked Mom, "Do you know anything about the Barrel Woman?"[1]

"Don't say that!" Mom knocked her tea over. She rushed to the kitchen.

Although I ducked around her for the sponge, she grabbed it first. I said to Mom's back, "But she was in the barrel, and she was an adult female, right?" I pulled out my phone and showed her a Reddit thread about Barrel Woman.

Mom mopped up the tea, red-faced and waving away my phone.

"She was a human being. We should speak of her with respect. That's why I work for the police, you know. We treat everyone with dignity and respect."

I raised my eyebrows instead of getting into another #BLM argument with her. "Okay, Mom. What should we call her, since she hasn't been identified yet?"

"The deceased," she told me immediately.

"But lots of people are dead, right? What if people got confused which dead person you meant?"

"Edan, you are so morbid. Have you been listening to those crime podcasts again?"

Of course I had. Callie threatened to buy me a true crime T-shirt for my birthday. "Sorry, Mom. Okay, do you know anything about the deceased?"

"I'm not a detective, Edan. I'm not even a police officer. How would I know anything?"

"You hear things," I stopped eyeballing her pink diary before she caught me. That shelf above the kitchen doorway used to hang out of reach, but I'm almost as tall as my mother now.

What had she written in her diary tonight? Could it have anything to do with the deceased?

Mom keeps a boring day timer too, but she saves the pink one for stuff about me, how far she ran last week (boring), how Garrett is "impenetrable" (I skip those parts). She hides her current diary, but I always suss it out in our one bedroom apartment. Once I found a mini diary in her tampon box.

"Don't be silly," said Mom. "I have enough work to keep me busy without eavesdropping on the officers."

"Then how did you know Officer Heather Peters had come in with me?"

"Edan!" She drank some more tea to calm herself. "They asked my permission, as your sole guardian. I messaged you that I'd come for your interview, which you would have known if you'd checked your messages."

"Sorry, Mom. I can't use my phone at school, and then I had to run to the police station."

"You should have checked it on the bus, but I bet you were talking to Callie, and you're always late." She shook her head. "You want to play cards, sweet pea?" she asked.

"No. I want to talk to Callie and Barstow."

"Why, were they with you at Red Rock?" She drew her white mug toward her and sipped it casually, like she wasn't trying to pimp me.

I matched her attitude. "Callie was. It's her birthday soon and she likes to hike, remember?"

"Yes, but wasn't Barstow sleeping over that night, too? I saw EBC when Garrett and I came home."

EBC means Edan, Barstow, and Callie. I blushed. I'm a terrible liar. "Yeah, but you know Barstow. He's not super into hiking."

"Neither are you. Did Callie invoke the birthday favor?"

Uh oh. My mom's not a cop, but she picks up way too much through osmosis, which we covered in science class last year.

"Callie and I like to do girls' night sometimes," I said, which is true.

"Before 8 a.m.?"

Oh, man. Maybe Mom is *worse* than a real cop.

"Girls' mornings are good too." I stuck to the truth as much as possible.

"Who knew you'd find a body? You're not even 14. I have to wonder if it runs in the family," she added under her breath.

I brightened. "You mean it happened to you?"

"No!"

I snapped my fingers. "Hold up. My dad found bodies too?" She won't tell me anything about my father. I assume he's Asian because I don't look mixed, and that he's reasonably tall because I'm already over five feet tall, like Mom. My mother gave me her own last name, Sze. How wild if this is the very first thing my dad passed on to me?

"I never said anything like that." Her phone buzzed, and she brightened. "Garrett finished earlier than he thought."

I made a face into my cup. She's been with Garrett for two years. He's basically a boring rectangular shape towering over my mom and me. He even has a square head. He's either working or working out. She says he's handsome, but I can't help staring at his nose (crooked because someone punched him and it didn't heal right) plus acne-scarred cheeks (please don't let that happen to me. We can't afford expensive medications on Mom's health care plan).

But it's really Garrett's personality. His next priorities, after working and working out, are tidiness and following the rules. Gross.

Now I had to help Mom set the table and get supper ready. Luckily, that meant cutting up red, yellow, and green peppers and arranging baby carrots while Mom steamed some frozen dumplings. Even if Garrett hints about his grandma's recipes, Mom never makes gross things like liver, which we both hate.

Garrett arrived in time to pile his plate with shrimp and pork dumplings and shove his legs under our mini table. "How'd you end up at Red Rock?"

I'd grabbed some dumplings before he'd cleaned out the steamer. I dunked mine in the hot sauce that he can't handle. "We found the barrel, so now we're implicated." That sounded official, even around a mouthful of pork.

His eyes slid toward Mom. "Your mom thought you went to the Red Rock Climbing Gym."

Oh. But I'd texted her a pic of the trail—

My eyes bulged. I'd sent a pic of more than the trail. I'd included me, Callie, and Barstow in front of the pinyon or juniper trees. So not only would my mom have figured out I'd gone to the real Red Rocks instead of the gym, but she also had photographic proof that both my friends had come with me.

"You okay? Too much hot sauce?" Garrett frowned at me.

"Yeah." I coughed into my hand, hiding my face. My mom obviously hadn't told Garrett everything. Why?

I couldn't figure that out now, so I smiled at him and changed the subject. "I'm investigating Red Rock as my summer project."

"Edan, no!" Mom exclaimed. She thinks I'm still her pigtailed six-year-old writing a prize-winning essay about how "Mommy+me=the perfect family" because "love is everything."

I all but folded my hands under my face and batted my eyes to look as kawaii (cute) as possible. "You said I could do anything I wanted this summer, before I have to work. This is my 'summer of freedom.'"[2]

Mom glowered. I knew that based on her own awesome memories, she'd imagined us seeing shows, exploring the Las Vegas Springs Preserve, and reading each other cool bits from our books. I want that too. I love my mom. But researching "the deceased" would be for *me*.

"That's not appropriate for someone your age." Garrett glared at me, his face flushed.

"Should I wait until I'm old?" I asked innocently, nibbling on the dumpling wrapper. By the way, I didn't turn red over the hot sauce. Unlike *some people*.

"Eighteen at least."

I nodded. "Just over four more years. I see."

Mom raised her eyebrows at me, exposing my secret sarcasm.

Garrett checked her face, then turned back to me. "This is serious business. Police business."

I nodded and dunked another dumpling in our delicious home-made hot sauce. My grandmother taught us how on a trip to Canada. The base ingredient is ketchup, believe it or not.

"You need years of training before you step into anything like this."

"Exactly. I want to become a police officer or a criminologist."

He eyed me up and down. I knew what he was thinking before he said it. "You'd need to work on the physical."

Yeah, no one mixes up my round body with Callie's muscles. "I can do that. But right now, I need to train my brain. I want to read about the case and figure out what's going on."

"That's for detectives."

"That's the kind of officer I want to be."

Garrett fumbled the filling from his dumpling, which plopped on the placemat. He fished for it with his chopsticks before my mom quietly laid a fork on the table for him.

Finally, he said, "You need any help, I'm here for you. I'll tell you what it's like to be an officer and what you need to do. As long as you're playing by the rules."

I seized a dumpling with my chopsticks and saluted him with it. "Thanks, Garrett. I love rules."

My mother cleared her throat. Shoot. I thought I'd turned my sarcasm level down to undetectable. Garrett glanced from me to my mom, still chewing.

Luckily, my phone buzzed with a text from Barstow.

Did you find $20 in my desk?

He keeps his emergency $20 in his homeroom desk. I remembered him pawing through his things this morning, but why would I have his money? Did he think I *stole* it?

EDAN

No

CALLIE

Me neither

BARSTOW

Ok, I'll keep looking

EDAN

I never even saw it. Didn't touch it

BARSTOW

I know

I scowled. Then why'd he ask? I crossed my arms. I hate being poorer than my friends. Other kids are like, *Can I borrow pizza money?* with Barstow, but I never do. I still owed him for the Wheelzz for Red Rock, although he insisted that was his birthday present to Callie.

Luckily, the next text punched that worry right out of my head.

CALLIE

> The police have called another press conference for tomorrow afternoon

BARSTOW

> I heard they id'd the body

CALLIE

> You think it's anyone we know?

I waited for Garrett to finish talking about his weight lifting breakthrough before I asked sweetly, "Is there any way I can go to the police press conference tomorrow?"

Garrett nearly spat out his yellow pepper.

5

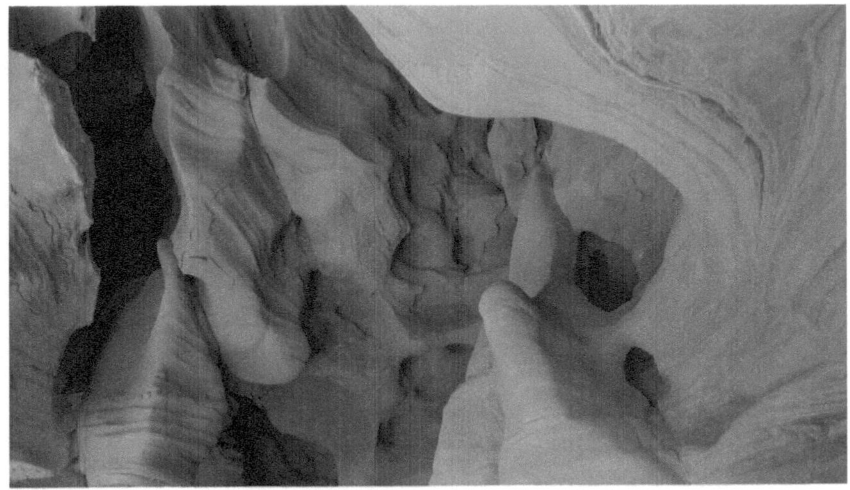

The next morning, I waved at Barstow and Callie through my apartment building's glass doors. Callie headed to the keypad to enter the passcode, but I yanked open my door first and called, "I can't believe Garrett forced me to go to school."

Mr. Villalobos's door flew open. "Quit banging on the toilet. It goes right down the pipes. I'll call the cops next time."

"Sorry, Mr. Villalobos," we all chorused, and I made sure both of my building's glass doors had sealed behind us before I rolled my eyes and reminded my friends, "Garrett is the *worst.*"

"Well, going to school is the law. And he is a police officer," said Barstow.

"Why are you taking his side?" I grumped.

"I'm not. I'm on logic's side."

"Forget logic. I want to go to the press conference."

Callie literally stepped between us.[1] "Okay. I know this is weird. But like my coach says, we've got to keep our head in the game."

"What game?" I wrinkled my nose.

"You want to figure out Barrel Woman's identity, right?"

"Right."

"You want to prove that you make a better cop than Garrett and your mom put together," she went on.

I ducked my head. "Am I that obvious?"

Callie and Barstow shared a look that translated as: yes, totes obvious.

I sighed and flung my arms apart. "Sor-ree."

"Don't get sorry. Go over, under, or through!" Callie called so loud that a pigeon fluttered off a phone wire.

I frowned at her. "Is that from Sesame Street or something?"

"Yes! But also Tina Fey talked about it in her autobiography, *Bossypants.* Whenever a stupid guy blocks her way, she thinks of Sesame Street and figures out how to get over, under, or through.[2]"

I cracked a grin. "Did you get that from Goodreads?"

"No, I read the book. Well, the audiobook. And you should too." She punched my arm harder than she should've.

I rubbed my arm to make the point. "Okay. You're right. I shouldn't whine. How do we go over, under, or through Garrett? And please don't make any jokes about my mom under him, or I'll barf."

"You don't need to go to the press conference," said Callie. "The news outlets will report everything anyway."

"Yes, but I want to a) see what a real press conference looks like, and b) check if anyone acts guilty. The killer could even come to the press conference. You know, to gloat."

Barstow frowned. "You mean like one of those serial killers who sent messages to the police to taunt them?"

"Exactly. Like ... Jack the Ripper!"

Callie raised her eyebrows.

I raised mine back. "I think there was someone more recent. Like the Zodiac Killer? I don't really know, though. My mom blocked my Internet searches."

"You want to search at my house, after we play Stardew?"[3] Barstow offered.

"Yes! Stardew Valley and search engines." Barstow has two computers *and* the fastest Wifi. I paused. "You won't get in trouble with your parents if I look for creepy stuff?"

He grinned. "I know how to get around blockers and erase a search history."

"It's more than clearing cookies," I warned him.

"I know that, Sze." He rolled his eyes at Callie.

"Hey." I elbowed both of them. "Well, as long as you're cool with it, yes, let's record the press conference if they stream it, and check out the cops and the audience."

"The audience will be the press," Callie pointed out.

"What if it's a journalist who did it?" My eyes saucered. "That's wild."

"Let's get logical about this," said Barstow. "The killer could be anyone, so we've got to narrow it down by means, motive, and opportunity."

"We don't know who it is and when it happened, so we can't narrow it down," I said.

He straightened his glasses. "Right. So there's no point in guessing now. All we can do is wait for the press conference and then plan our next move."

Barstow's one of my best friends. Good thing, or I'd strangle him when he's too infuriatingly logical.

"Unless we figured out who it was first," said Callie thoughtfully. "We could go through the missing persons records."

Barstow cackled. "How many people go missing in Vegas every day?"

I was afraid to Google it, but I did. "Five to seven adults a day, which makes over 200 a month. Plus 8000 kids a year."

"Ouch," said Callie. "I knew it would be a lot, but that's ... ouch."

We all sat on a nearby bench for a second, between gum and someone's abandoned Starbuck's cup, imagining those people vanishing and why.

"Good thinking outside the box, though," said Barstow, and we fist-bumped Callie simultaneously before we started walking again.

She smiled. "All Edan's idea."

"Aww." We'd hug it out if we were that type of crew, but we save hugs for special occasions because Barstow's not into touching "unless someone's dying."

One good thing, they moved the press conference to 3 p.m., right at the end of school. We hoofed it to the bleachers while listening to Barstow's phone, which is so good that it hardly glitched all the way through the press conf introductions.

I recognized the Black cop from our visit, Mark Evans. He thanked the audience and told us how far their police department had come.

"The LVPD has made headway into the identity of the deceased found at the Red Rock Canyon. Officer Heather Peters will give you further information."

The deceased, just like my mom said. Maybe she even suggested they say that, although I don't know if they'd take press conference advice from a secretary. She's not a police officer or media whiz, so she jokes that she's the bottom of the barrel.

Heather Peters stepped up to the microphone. "We have spoken to the family and are now ready to reveal the identity in hopes that it will help further our case. The deceased was a strong member of our community and will be greatly missed. The principal of Forester Middle School was also a wife, a mother who sang in her church choir. We offer our condolences to the family, friends, and students of Gretel Linkletter."[4]

6

"*Mrs. Linkletter?*" I burst out. "Our principal? No way!"

"Shh!" Callie grabbed my arm, and I bit my lip hard enough to draw blood.

Up 'til now, it had seemed like a movie or video game. Sure, we found the barrel, but we never looked inside. We didn't even touch it. But now. Now. I *knew* Mrs. Linkletter. She said hi to every kid, which is kind of impossible in a school with 2000 students, but she tried. She'd call out, "Edan, Barstow, and Callie." Then she'd sing out "E-B-C" and count, to the tune of a song called ABC.[1]

Why would anyone hurt her?

"The LVPD has sealed off Red Rock Canyon to visitors for further investigation," Officer Peters announced on screen.

That meant we couldn't go in. Not that I wanted to. What if we ran into the killer?

But what if the killer was at our school?

"Who'd kill Mrs. Linkletter?" Callie whispered.

"Shh!" Barstow pointed at our screen.

Callie hugged her knees and rocked back and forth. I rubbed her back, but she didn't seem to feel me. Goosebumps pimpled her arms.

Even though Barstow didn't speak, I could read the tension in his neck and arms.

"At the moment, the LVPD recommends caution. It would be prudent to buddy up. Do not approach the Red Rock Canyon area until our investigation is complete. Children should not be left unsupervised. We will keep the public informed. If you have any information, please call our hotline. You could win a reward."

When we wandered back into the school, most people seemed to know already. One girl, Ava, sobbed near her locker. "She was so nice. She cared about my goldfish."[2]

"Foresters, please," Mr. Eisen's voice trembled over the speaker. "We've had some shocking news. Today we learned that our fearless principal, Mrs. Linkletter, was found deceased."

That word again. I clung to that, and to my friends' hands, one on each side. Barstow had broken his own rule by touching us. Then I realized, no. He saved touch for when someone died, and we'd lost Mrs. Linkletter.

"We will never forget Mrs. Linkletter. Please come to the office if you need to talk to someone, or to call your parents to pick you up."

I squeezed Barstow's chilly hand, but he let go and straightened up, pushing his glasses up his nose.

Callie interlaced her fingers with mine.

"You okay?" I whispered.

She nodded and whispered back, "Sort of. I'm worried about Barstow."

"He didn't cry," I said. Barstow still wore almost no expression, like he couldn't hear us.[3]

"That's why I'm worried. She and his mom were friends. He knew her better than we did."

Oh, right. My mom doesn't have time for the Parent Teacher Association. Mr. and Mrs. Yang don't either, because they wrangle Callie to swimming and whatnot.

Barstow's mom, though ... "Isn't Mrs. Ness the president of the PTA?"

Callie nodded.

Barstow turned to me, suddenly fierce. "I'm in."

"I know."

"No. I was riding along because we found the barrel. But now—" His Adam's apple bobbed up and down. "Mrs. Linkletter didn't deserve that. I'm going to catch whoever did this and nail him to the wall."

7

We circled the hallways until I said, "I hear you, Barstow. Regroup."

"How do you mean?" Callie asked.

"On crime podcasts, they take a step back to figure out what we know before we keep going." And also to drag Barstow back to logic. I'd never seen him this mad. We walked past two girls whispering to each other at our lockers. I pointed at our history classroom. "Can we go back in there?"

Callie pushed open the door. "Oh, sorry, Mr. Carver!"

Our history teacher swivelled to face us. Hard to tell under his usual beard, but I thought he looked pale.

He still held the chalk in his hand from writing tomorrow's quote, *War is a lottery in which nations ought to risk nothing but small amounts— Napoleon, 1769-1821, French Emperor*

"Are you okay?" I asked Mr. Carver.

He shook his head, then nodded, then shook his head again before he dropped his chalk. I guess even teachers didn't know what to do. Mr. Carver teaches and runs the athletic department, but had probably never run into anything like this before.

I tried to cheer him up by reminding him of history while I scooped up the chalk. "Kind of like the Civil War, where you're surrounded by 'traitors, spies, smugglers, robbers and house burners,' right, Mr. Carver?"

Mr. Carver didn't seem to hear me. He stayed frozen in place until I nudged his fingers with the chalk, and he took it back automatically.

A kid named Vernon rushed in behind us. "Can I plug in my phone? I need to call my mom."

"Vernon!" Mr. Carver spun around with his arms outstretched.

I lunged away from Mr. Carver, but somehow still bumped into him and then Vernon, who gasped, "Watch it, E-Z!" before I teetered into a four-legged splat at Vernon's feet.

Callie gasped, but I caught myself on the cool tile floor using both hands, stinging my palms and embarrassing the heck out of me.[1]

"I'm so sorry, Edan." Mr. Carver gave me a hand up, looking horrified behind his red beard.

"No problem." I showed him my palms—no blood—and he mimed wiping his forehead with relief before he waved Vernon over to the power outlet. Meanwhile, I really did rub my hands on my jeans to get rid of Mr. Carver's palm sweat. Yuck.

"Poor Vernon," said Callie, but not too loud. Vernon had a crush on her last year and stared at her until she switched seats to try and get out of his range of vision. "Where should we go?"

"How about the music room?" I suggested. I play the flute, and Ms. Williams is pretty cool about letting us rehearse.

"Sounds as good as anywhere else," said Barstow, and Callie nodded.

I knocked on the door and pushed it open. "Hello?"

Someone had turned off the lights. We entered through the narrow hall, hurrying past the shelves holding student instruments.[2]

"Where's the light switch?" Barstow grumbled.

I fumbled up and down on the wall on my right until I managed to hit the switch. Fluorescent lights slowly blinked into life above us.

I landed on the hard plastic chair in the main room, third row and near the right, where I usually played my flute. No music filled the music stands, which seemed fitting.

Barstow paced. "What's the point of having a pow wow. We don't know anything. We need to get out there!"

"We can't go back to Red Rock. Police orders," Callie pointed out. "Where would we go?"

"I don't know. Anywhere, I don't care!"

Barstow never lost his cool. I traced my way up to the elevated back row, where the tuba player and the drummer usually took up space on the opposite side of the room. Callie sat at the piano, feet on the bench, hugging her knees again. My music teacher would hate the footprints, but I bet Mrs. Williams would give us a break right now.

"When was the last time one of us saw Mrs. Linkletter?" I asked them. "She didn't do the morning announcements yesterday, but before then?"

Callie's brow crinkled. "I have swimming Monday-Wednesday-

Friday. I come to school early and sometimes I see her. Saw her," she added softly. "I can't remember if I walked past her on Friday."

"Thursday was PTA night," Barstow cut in.

"Did you see her? Like, I don't know if you meet at your houses?" I asked. I never cared about the Parent Teacher Association before.

Barstow snorted. "They usually have 'em at school. There's more room, and the school passes out coffee and muffins."

"So you didn't go?" I asked him.

"For some reason, Mrs. L asked to hold it outside the school. My mom offered our place and took over our living room. I hid in my room, so I don't know if Mrs. Linkletter came or not." He hesitated before he texted his mom. "Ah, she's upset about Mrs. L, hang on."

That reminded me to text my mom too.

EDAN

> I'm fine. Don't worry. I'll be home soon.

MOM

I'll come get you!

EDAN

> Please no

MOM

I'll ask Garrett

EDAN

> OMG MOM NO

MOM

I'm worried.

EDAN

> Callie and Barstow are here

MOM

Where are you??????

EDAN

in the music room

MOM

You should lock the door

EDAN

We're not allowed to lock it

MOM

EDAN SZE YOU DO WHAT I SAY

I clicked the door lock closed and prayed that Mrs. Williams wouldn't break it down and kick our butts.

"Mrs. Linkletter did come to the meeting at our house," Barstow reported. "Mom says that Mrs. L seemed upset and kind of distracted, but 'always professional.'"

"Hmm. We need more details," I told him.

"I'm trying!" He kept texting, then lifted his head. "Mom'll think about it. She's too upset to talk."

Grown ups. Or groan ups. I bit my tongue and said, "Good job."

Callie smiled at me. She gives me tips on handling "groan ups." Like never insulting them. Adults criticize us all the time, but hey. We need to take it and say yes, ma'am. Don't even think of pointing out that their room is messier than your sofa bed. Does not go over well. Ask me how I know.[3]

Callie changed the subject. "If they recorded the PTA meeting, we might be able to figure it out for ourselves. Maybe Mrs. L dropped some clues!"

"Right," said Barstow. "Someone would have taken minutes. I doubt anyone did an audio recording, but I could ask. Thanks, Cal."

"We might pick up something they didn't," I agreed. "Let's think about this. We want to know why she was upset. If she let anything slip."

"And what time the meeting started and ended," said Barstow. "We need to trace her whereabouts."

"Did Mrs. L make it to school on Friday?" I tapped my heel on the green carpet. "Did any of us see her? I'm pretty sure I didn't."

Barstow wrinkled his forehead. "No, I don't think so."

"Wait. Friday, I set a personal best in the backstroke," said Callie. "I went to tell Ms. Hernandez, because she used to coach swimming and likes to know how it's going. Mrs. Linkletter's door was closed, and the 'Back at' clock was still pointing at 8 a.m."

We all stared at each other.

Finally, I spoke up. "That means either she came late, or—"

"Or she never showed up at all." Barstow smacked his forehead. "Which means she was last seen at that PTA meeting!"

8

"Oh, hi, Garrett," I said, freezing mid-body roll.

That evening, after coming home from school, I'd needed to dance. Mr. Villalobos had complained about my elephant feet as I practiced the 1 Million dance choreography to Rema's song "Calm Down,"[1] so I'd taken my moves outside—only to run into my mom's boyfriend.

Garrett waved and continued lathering up his headlight in front of our apartment. He'd attached a hose to our outdoor spigot. Garrett liked to wash his car in a certain way, by hand.

I thought we should conserve water in the desert. Also the temperature outside was 98 degrees, even at 7 p.m. Mr. Villalobos might split in half if he came out and saw a non-resident using up our precious H2O.[2]

But instead of pointing that out, I decided to pick Garrett's police brain. "I was wondering if you have any more information about that case?"

"About what?" He lifted a soapy rag to polish the car's window frame.

"The case of the deceased at Red Rock." He stared at me, so I added, "You know, the woman who was, uh, found in a barrel."

He laid down his rag and focused on me for the first time. "You should concentrate on school."

"School ends next Friday."

"I'm sure you could learn a lot no matter what time of year. Instead of goofing off with your friends, you could hit the library. That's one of my regrets. I should have made the most of my education. Not that I don't learn every day on the force. I'm not saying that."

"Of course not," I said. "Sure, that's a good idea. I like the library."

He raised his eyebrows, and too late, I realized that he knew me well enough to figure out that I wouldn't cave that easily. He went on, "Not for reading romance books or anything like that. Nothing made up."

What a Garrett. I downloaded romances, mysteries, fantasy, science fiction, and horror—every single thing made up—every day on my phone, with at least two different apps. I remembered Callie's parental advice though, so I widened my eyes and shook my head. "I get that, but I want to concentrate on real stuff right now. Like Red Rock."

He picked up his rag and worked on a headlight. "I can't tell you nothing. Everything is confidential."

Man. What is the point of your mother dating a cop if he won't help you out, even a teaspoon?

"Don't look so disappointed, Edan. I did one thing for you even before you asked. I told your mother you're probably all curious because you've got questions about your own life."

I blinked at him while he picked up the windshield wiper so he could clean under it.

"That's right," he said, laying the wiper back against the glass with great care. "She promised me that tonight, she'd answer your questions about your biological father."

"My *father?*" I choked out.

Mom had clammed up every time I quizzed her about him. I didn't know his first name, where he came from, or where he took off to. Nada.

Garrett set the wiper back down. "I've seen a lot in my time, and in my experience, people never stop looking for what's missing. In your case, no wonder you focused ina—inappropriately on Red Rock. Now let's redirect your energy to your own past so you can move on with your life."

I barely heard him. *My father! My father! My father!* whirled in my brain.

"Hey, what'cha doing there?" shouted Mr. Villalobos, who'd pushed open the building's front door.

"Washing my car," said Garrett.

"You can't do that stuff on our property. You're not even on the lease."

"Just doing some detail work." Garrett squared off against the much older and smaller man.

"You're right, Mr. Villalobos. Garrett was finishing up, weren't you, Garrett?" I asked.

After a long minute, Garrett's chin dipped in agreement. "I hardly used any water."

"Even one drop of water is too much in the desert, you big lug."

"We're so sorry, Mr. Villalobos," I said, and eventually I managed to guide our neighbor to the double doors.

After Mr. Villalobos finally retreated inside his apartment, grumbling, I headed up the flight of stairs to our own place and locked the door behind me. While I grabbed a glass of water, I tried to put together the pieces of my own personal mystery.

My mom never changed her last name. "I was a feminist. Still am," she told me, when I asked her about it. So she grew up as Amy Sze, and she passed her last name to me, which is legit. But it also took away one big clue to help find my dad. Even my birth certificate didn't list a father.

I know he didn't stick around. *Wham, bam, oh, hello, baby, let me give you the Celtic name for fire to make sure that you have two names no one can pronounce.*

I love my mom and her family. I meant it when I wrote that essay half a lifetime ago that we were a family and didn't need anything else. When other kids teased me, sure, I cried when I was little. But after a few years, with Barstow and Callie at my side, I couldn't care less. Single parent family? Not exactly the first one in the USA.

Sure, I wondered if Dad passed on my relatively narrow eyes or slightly wavy hair. If someone said, "You from the Philippines? You got the right skin," I'd say, "I'm American." Easier to shake off the "But where are you *really* from?" losers than explain that I can't pinpoint my parents' original countries. Sze is Chinese, but who knew where the other half of my DNA formed before heading to Nevada?

I learned to live with not knowing.

Maybe Garrett had a point. I needed extra answers because I didn't know my father, and part of me was sick of secrets.

A key scraped in our lock, turning the bolt.

I yelped even before the door banged open. Like, what if talking about my dad actually brought him to our apartment after almost 14 years?

"Dad?" I whispered.

9

"Dad, is that you?" I crouched against the wall of the living room, almost ready to jump into our tiny bathroom to the right of the front door.

My mother stared back at me, her face blank. "He told you."

"Who told me what?" I asked Mom, silently instructing my stomach to stop jumping.

"Garrett." Mom kicked off her shoes without making sure to stack them neatly by the front door. Then she locked the door and tossed her bag on the floor. "He made me promise to tell you about your father."

I licked my lips. Mom was keeping her promise to Garrett. I didn't want to mess up the moment, so I started with the basics. "What's his name?"

"Eddie." She screwed up her face, forcing herself to keep going. "Edward Wong."

"Eddie." The name felt strange coming out of my mouth. After over a decade of complete silence, my mom handed me my bio dad's name. It seemed crazy, though. No one is named Eddie. Except me, sort of. "You named me after him?"

"No, your name is Celtic for fire." She paused. "Also, maybe a little. I swear, it didn't occur to me until I filled out the birth certificate. But he never came looking for you, so I guess it's okay." She pointed to the kitchen on my left. "I need coffee."

"Okay."

She grabbed a jar of instant from the cupboard to the right of the sink. Wow, she couldn't wait for coffee to perk. She added two cubes of brown sugar (also serious—two cubes!) and milk before I tackled the next question.

"Why is it good that he never came looking for me? Is he a criminal?"

Mom burst out laughing. "Absolutely not." She took two more sips, still chuckling.

I relaxed a little.

"He's a lawyer. Or he was. If he'd known about you, he might have tried to take you away from me. I couldn't let him do that." Every hint of humor scraped off her face. I swear the room temperature dropped two degrees.

"So he doesn't know I exist?"

She turned her dark eyes on me. "Not unless you tell him."

Wild. I couldn't process that right now. "Do you have contact information for him?"

She shook her head. "After he left, he never contacted me again."

My throat tightened. I had to think about it, but I knew that wasn't the same thing. "He didn't contact you, but do you know how to contact him? Like, maybe through social media?"

"No. I was glad he left."

I shook my head. "Why? You can't have been happy about raising a crying baby on your own."

"He was too strict. His parents believed in following the rules, so he did, too. Not only the law, but once I left the house wearing one brown sock and one orange sock,[1] and he made me go home to change."

I tried to imagine Strict Eddie raising me. "That sounds horrible."

"He wasn't like that at first, but the closer he got to graduation, the more he wanted to do everything 'right.' He needed a woman who cared as much, or more, than he did, about those things." She shrugged and sipped her coffee. "Lots of times, I wished I could."

Made me want to run the other way, but what do I know, I've never dated anyone, or wanted to.

"I was an actor," she said softly. "We met after my show, when his friends dragged him to the same bar. He said I was luminous and he couldn't resist me."

I shook my head like a dog flinging water out of my ear canals. "You were an actor?" *A luminous actor? What?*

"I didn't dream about typing up reports and press releases." She smiled at me. "But when I realized you were on your way, I had to earn money, not memorize monologues and go to auditions that would either result in 'not for us' or get me a job for 'exposure.'"[2]

My eyes bugged out. "They wanted you to strip for casinos on The Strip?"

"No, honey. 'Exposure' is code for not paying you, so you do the job for free publicity." She grinned. "I never had to strip."

"Thank God."

"Although now I wish I'd—"

I covered my ears. "La la la la la la."

Once her mouth stopped moving, I removed my hands, and she laughed some more before washing a bunch of green grapes and popping one in her mouth.

I rolled a grape between my thumb and index finger. "Does he still live in Las Vegas?"

She shook her head "He couldn't wait to leave. He didn't want to work in entertainment law."

I bet Mr. Matchy Socks didn't. "What kind of law did he choose?"

"He was interested in tax and corporate law. But I don't know where he went, honestly. We ... fell out on a trip, and later I found out I was expecting you. He didn't reach out, and I haven't heard from him since." She crossed her heart in front of me and whispered, "Hope to die."

"Don't say that, Mom." I'm a bit superstitious. I don't like hearing stuff like that.

"Sorry, baby." She ruffled my hair, and I leaned against her for a minute, like I used to when I was little.

My heart thumped in my chest.

I had a dad. A real, honest to God father who didn't know me. I could search for him and figure out where I came from, biologically. I could uncover a whole half of my family tree who had no idea I existed.

Or I could keep asking about Red Rock.

Which one first?

10

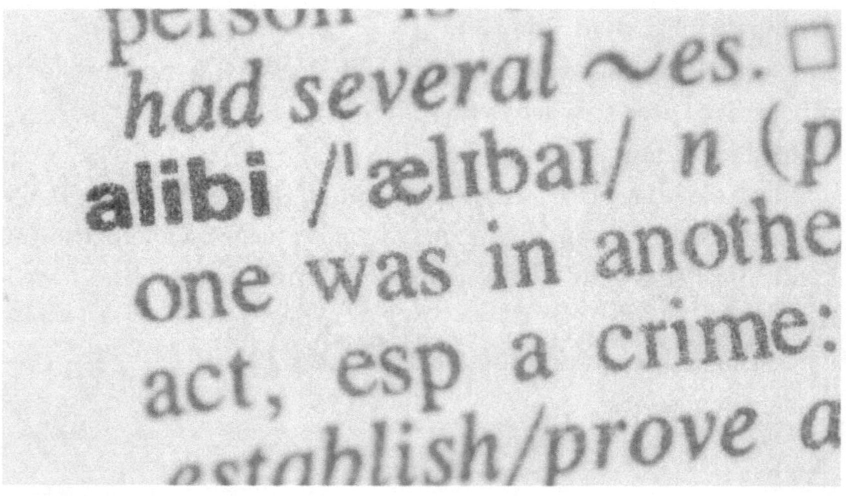

"A lawyer?" Barstow raised his eyebrows in his window on Mom's laptop, which she'd lended me because it ran video calls better than my old phone.

"Not a lawyer!" Callie mimicked The Scream, or maybe the Home Alone hands-to-cheeks meme, in her window beside Barstow's on my screen.

For the first time, I laughed at these factoids about my bio dad. "I know, I was shocked too. I mean, shocked enough to call you."

Callie recovered first. "Why not a lawyer? You're persuasive, and you don't stop."

I didn't see that so much, but maybe it's like how Barstow's nose always seemed normal until Gary MacLean started holding up his knuckle beside his nose to imitate our friend last year. In retaliation, Callie and I tossed garbage on Gary's bike after he left it outside overnight. His parents grounded him for not taking care of it, and Gary had to scrape banana peel off his spokes instead of bugging Barstow.[1]

"Let me see if I can track your dad down for you," said Barstow.

"I started to, but got over 78 million hits for Edward Wongs in the U.S. And what if he went to Canada or another country? People move for work, especially if they're ambitious enough to worry about socks." I shuddered.

"Leave it with me. I like digging," said Barstow.

"If you want. Thanks." For a minute, I couldn't talk past the lump in my throat, so Callie told us about her non-existent swimming lesson after someone messed up the chlorine levels.

"That's whacked." I cleared my throat. "Any more news about Mrs. L, while we're at it?"

"Definitely not at school all of Friday," said Callie. "I asked Mrs. Hernandez. Mrs. Linkletter never showed."

"Hmm. So that means we were right. She was last seen alive at the Thursday PTA meeting. Any more intel from your mom?" I asked Barstow.

"A little. Mrs. L moved the meeting time to 4 p.m. and left a bit early, like a bit after five."

"That's when she drove away?"

He frowned and shook his head. "I didn't see her drive away. She has the silver Honda Civic with the flower stickers."

I couldn't help smiling for a second. Nobody can miss Mrs. Linkletter's car, even in Vegas traffic. "Did you see her car?"

Barstow shook his head.

"Who came, anyway?" I asked.

Barstow rolled his eyes. "My mom didn't take roll call, but I remembered who she mentioned. I'll send you both a list."

"Thank ye." I pretended to curtsey, even if it got lost over video. "They might be the last people to see Mrs. L alive. Did the police question your mom?"

Barstow nodded. "They asked her to come to the station."

"And your mom still doesn't know what you were doing on Saturday?"

He looked upset. "They get my Wheelzz receipts."

Oh. Oh, crap. Barstow had paid for everything, including our trip there and back. I had no idea if a location showed up on those receipts, but ...

"You could have paid for it and not come," Callie pointed out.

Barstow managed a one second smile. "The driver would remember me."

"Do you share your driving location with your parents too?" I didn't know much about it, since I take the bus or walk or bike.

Barstow winced before he checked his settings on the app. "Yeah. It's a safety thing."

"So your parents know that you went to Red Rock." Maybe it didn't matter that my mom knew if the Nesses did too.

He lifted his shoulders. "If they check the location services, or if they go into my receipts. They haven't done it yet. But maybe they will now that my mom's talking to the police."

"Unless they already know and don't mind," said Callie. "We didn't do anything wrong. We reported a barrel. Good thing we did."

Barstow shook his head. "If the cops figure out I was at Red Rock, they'll question me. Hard. And what about my mom? My mom hosted Mrs. Linkletter Thursday night, and I pointed out the barrel on Saturday. Even I find it sus."

"Sus," we agreed, subdued. Suspicious as heck. *We* knew Barstow hadn't done anything, but what would the cops believe?

"You have an alibi, though, right?" I asked him.

Barstow nearly chocked on a laugh. "What are you saying?"

"Let's talk about Thursday, when Mrs. L went missing. We should all have alibis. Just smart, you know what I mean?"

"I know," said Callie, flashing me a small smile. "Thursday, I have piano, and then my dad drove me home to have dinner and crash. Friday, I woke up early for swimming, did school with you two, then slept over at your place until Saturday, Edan."

"Excellent. Barstow?"

He shook his head. "After school Thursday, you and I played Stardew Valley. I ate in my room because of the PTA meeting. Then I did my homework, fell asleep, and did school on Friday, and ended up at your sleepover."

Really not as good a Thursday alibi as Callie's. "Did your parents check on you?" I asked.

"My mom brought my supper. And you played Terraria with me after homework too." He knew why I asked.

Callie cut in. "Were any of your assignments online, on Docs? They would have time stamps in the cloud, if you looked hard enough."

He shook his head. "I worked on a song for part of it, playing guitar and drums."

"Out loud, where your parents could hear?"

"I used my headphones. You know it's an electric guitar and drum kit. My parents got it for me on purpose, so I wouldn't disturb them."

Crap crap crap crap crap. "I'm sure we'll think of something. Anyway, you were home. No one would have seen you leave your house, and you're only 13 years old. I'm being paranoid. Sorry."

"I guess." Barstow started drumming to relieve tension.

"What about your Thursday to Friday?" Callie asked me.

I had to think. "Stardew ... I think Barstow and me played until 4ish. At least my mom yelled at me to get off. I didn't know Barstow was eating, but maybe that's why we got rocked on the skull caverns."[2]

"I didn't eat at the skull caverns," he said. "And who got the prismatic shard, huh?"

"You *always* get the prismatic shard." Seriously, I've only scooped up one out of five so far, and Barstow held back so I could scoop that shard.[3] I crinkled my forehead. "I danced with the Fitness Marshall."

Callie laughed. Even Barstow cracked a grin.

"It's quality music, and Marshall's hilarious," I defended myself. "I wasn't ready to do my homework, so I went for a walk." I'd almost forgotten about that.

"Okay. Where did you go?" Callie asked.

"Well. Mr. Villalobos yelled at me—"

We all sighed at that.

"—then I headed toward Barstow's house. He wasn't answering his texts."

Barstow sat up. "You didn't tell me that."

"What time was your walk?" asked Callie.

"I'm trying to remember. After five for sure. I thought we had time for a few rounds of Stardew before I headed back."

"So you walked to my house around the time that the PTA meeting was breaking up," Barstow said.

I bit my lip, still putting it together. "Right. You had so many people at your place, I turned around. One woman looked a bit like Mrs. L, but I've never seen her in this eggplant dress."

Barstow wrinkled his forehead. "I think she wore a long purple thing, not her work clothes. And some big necklace too."

Callie and I exchanged looks.

"Did anyone else wear a dress to that meeting?" I asked Barstow.

"I don't know." He thought about it. "Maybe my mom. She's got this one with tiger stripes that she jokes about making her a tiger mom."

"Long skirt?" Callie asked him.

"No, it's short. She always says that she looks fierce."

His fit mom looks nothing like round Mrs. L, even without the tiger stripes. "I must've seen Mrs. Linkletter. Okay."

"You're killing us! What was she doing?" Callie clapped her hands together.

I tried to remember. "She was getting into a car. Maybe an SUV? It didn't look like a flowery Honda Civic to me."

Callie slapped the air in front of her. I swear that she would have hit me if we'd been sitting together. "Edan, YOU might be the last person who saw Mrs. Linkletter alive. You have to talk to the police!"

11

"Report this," Callie insisted. "If they don't believe you, it's their loss."

Barstow stayed mute.

I wished I knew how to crack my knuckles. Anything to relieve the tension. "Yeah, but I don't have any information except Mrs. Linkletter's dress and the time I saw her. How does that help?"

Callie's eyes gleamed. "I'm going to hypnotize you."

"What?"

Barstow snapped his fingers. "I've heard about this. It's legit."[1]

I shook my head. "Okay, I've heard of hypnosis too, but do you know how to hypnotize people? It's for people who know what they're doing."

"I've read about it a lot. I didn't tell you guys because, well, it's weird. Also, people don't know whether to trust you if you have hypnotic powers, even though consent is always part of a respectful hypnotist's arsenal."

Huh? We both stared at her.

Callie faced me. "I need your permission. I wouldn't do it otherwise. But you know that your conscious mind is blocking information, right? You didn't even know you'd seen Mrs. L until now. Talk about a brain block! I can take you back to the moment it happened. You'll describe it to me and Barstow. We'll record it."

"I don't know," I said slowly.

Barstow held up his hand. "Yeah. I have a feeling that the police will freak if we do this. You're not a real hypnotist, Callie. You're a kid. When they see that you've hypnotized a key witness, that could throw the whole case in jeopardy."[2]

"We don't have to tell them the hypnosis part. If Edan comes up with anything useful, amazing. If she doesn't, no harm done, right? Unless you want her to run to the police right now?"

Barstow made a face. "I never said that. But we don't want to tamper with evidence. Memories are evidence, even if they're flawed."

"Hey now." My hands formed fists, and my teeth ground together.

Barstow held up his hand. "I'm not saying you're a liar, Edan. I know you. But they've done eyewitness studies that basically show that it's garbage. We think we know and we remember, but we don't. It's almost the same as chance. Worse than chance, because we end up making up information and imprisoning the wrong person. That happens all the time."

"Right. Especially to people of colour." The three of us knew this even before we did a project on the criminal justice system. I let go of my anger and sighed. "Okay."

"You're still my main girl. Both of you," he told Callie.

"I need to think about this. I could be the last person who saw Mrs. Linkletter alive." I swallowed. "That means maybe she'd still be alive today if I'd stopped her."

Callie shook her head hard enough to loosen some of her hair from her braid. "Don't go there. Why would you run up to someone and stop her from getting into a car? She wasn't calling for help, right?"

"No, I would have noticed that."

Barstow exhaled. "She made her own choices."

"She didn't ask to be killed."

"She didn't ask you to save her, either."

We both had to give each other some breathing room. I closed my eyes and whispered, "Okay."

"Okay, I should hypnotize you?" Callie clapped her hands in her screen window.

"No, okay that I'll give the police a call. Even if I'm almost as scared as—" I almost said Barstow, but he scowled at me, and I switched it to "Zenitsu Agatsuma."

They both gazed at me, totally blank. I sighed at them. "You've got to brush up on your anime. When this is all over, I demand a watch party for *Demon Slayer: Kimetsu no Yaiba*. Then you'll know who Zenitsu is."

I counted on a future where we could watch anime instead of searching for a killer.

12

Barstow texted us an hour later, after I got back home.

That was all. But we both knew what it meant. Mrs. Linkletter had changed into a dress for the PTA meeting. I probably really had seen her last, out of everyone in Las Vegas, except for her killer.

CALLIE

I knew it!

EDAN

OMG

Why didn't I realize it was Mrs. Linkletter at the time? I'm not someone who stares at other people. Even though I told Garrett I want to become a police officer, I'd have to knuckle down on my observation skills.

I decided to go for a walk again. Not everyone realizes that Las Vegas is way more than The Strip. Sure, that's where tourists go to party and gamble and eat at buffets, but most of us are normal people going to school and working and stuff.

I walked past a high rise where someone had abandoned a pair of sweat pants.[1] I cracked a smile. Yeah, gross, but very Vegas too.

I kept walking and thinking. Everyone knew Mrs. Linkletter's car. Not only was it a silver Honda Civic, but she'd pasted a bunch of flower and butterfly decals all over the body. Some people thought it looked lame, like she should teach at an elementary school instead middle school, but I kind of liked it. She had three bumper stickers, one for our school, one for Gamblers Anonymous, and another one for a butterfly garden.

I strolled past a clinic. In the alleyway, someone had abandoned a sign that said, in bubble letters, PLEASE HELP. GOD BLESS.[2]

Yep, I could use some help and some blessing, even though I'm not religious. I kept walking and thinking. On Thursday, when that SUV had passed a stoplight, I hadn't spotted any butterflies, flowers, or bumper stickers.

What about the license plate?

I closed my eyes and smelled car exhaust. A man walked past me in dirty clothes. I waited until he passed, then closed my eyes again, desperately trying to visualize.

Nevada plate, I thought. *And maybe a 8 and an A?*

I texted my crew, who replied immediately.

CALLIE

That's amazing!

BARSTOW

u sure

No, I wasn't sure. But I had to call the police anyway, now that this might lead to the killer. I headed home to call in peace and privacy.

The police number sent me to voice mail.

I left a message, but no one called me back before school the next morning. I kept checking my phone as we lingered on the school steps, not wanting to hide it in my locker when the police might reach out.

"It doesn't matter if they call you back right away. The important thing is that you reported it," Callie told me.

Barstow nodded. "Now they have the information, and they've got the resources to check license plates and talk to other witnesses, including the PTA moms. It's out of your hands. You did your job."

The bell rang, but Callie put out her hand to stop me from heading to homeroom. "If you want to try hypnosis, though, I'll give it a try."

I glanced at Barstow, who looked like he was thinking about it.

So was I. "How did you learn hypnosis again?"

"Off YouTube. I read a book too."

"And you don't think you'll mess up my brain?"

"No! All I do is make suggestions. You decide what you want to do with it. Even under hypnosis, you make decisions and set limits."

"Then why do I see hypnotized people playing their feet like banjos and stuff like that?" I asked.

She grinned. "You did look it up then."

"A little."

"The hypnotist walks you into your subconscious. I can plant a suggestion and an end point. You know how some of them are like, your hands are stuck together and you won't be able to pull them apart until I snap my fingers?"

"I've seen a couple like that." Barstow laughed.

Meanwhile, Callie shook her head. "I'll suggest that when I clap my hands, you'll come out. Barstow can watch and record you. Nothing to worry about."

"Unless I never come out," I said. "What if something happens to you, and I'm trapped in Thursday night forever, watching a woman climb into a car?"[3]

Callie's brow wrinkled. "I think I can make it so that you'll come out if me *or* Barstow clap our hands. So even if something happened to me, you'd have a backup."

"What if something happens to both of you, like a bomb?"

"Then we're all dead! Seriously. Okay, what if I make it so if you hear any loud noise like a clap or a *bomb*, you'll snap out of it?"

"Better." I turned to Barstow while we walked toward the classroom. "What do you think?"

"I can also set a timer to go off. That way you have another fail safe."

"All of our timers," I said. I really hate losing control. I want to be the one in charge. "Okay. And where would we do it?"

"Anywhere you feel comfortable," Callie said. "You want to do it at your apartment?"

I shook my head. No privacy. I slept in the living room. Callie's little sister listens at our door sometimes. Which directed us to one place only. "Barstow's."

"Good choice," she said.

"I'm game," said Barstow. "I'll text my parents."

"Great." But my heart rapped in my chest. I'd look up hypnosis every spare second today. I was letting her into my brain based on a YouTube video.

In the distance, I heard my phone playing "Ike Iko." Somehow, I knew that Officer Heather Peters summoned me to the police station after school.

13

After school, I headed into the police station. Callie couldn't miss a practice. Barstow had taken the bus with me and nodded at me when I got off.

You can do this, I told myself as I signed in with the police station's air conditioning blasting my face.[1] *Tell the cops and leave.*

Five minutes later, Officer Peters ushered me and Mom into a small, windowless private room. Like the last time, we sat in white plastic chairs cemented to the floor, and at least two cameras pointed at us.

"Don't be nervous. Look at me and tell me what you remember," Officer Peters rasped, and I realized she might've worn out her voice over the past 72 hours.[2]

I tried to ignore the cameras and the fluorescent lights as I gave her the info. Afterward, I realized that I'd picked out a bunch of threads from the bottom of my jean shorts onto the floor while talking. I didn't want to crawl around picking them up, so I ignored them. Mom glanced at the floor but didn't comment.

"Why didn't you give us this information before?" asked Officer Peters. She sat across from us with a pad of yellow paper and a pen, taking notes.

"I didn't know it was important before. When we reported the barrel, it could've been empty." *Be calm like Barstow.* "On Monday, we heard there was a body, but we only got the identity yesterday. That night, we figured out I'd seen Mrs. Linkletter at the end of her PTA meeting, getting into a car, wearing different clothes from school."

She frowned. "Let's back it up. What was Mrs. Linkletter wearing at school?"

"I don't remember, but I'm pretty sure it was pants and a shirt."

"That's all. You don't know the kind or color?"

I shook my head.

"Shoes?"

"No, sorry. I'm not into fashion."

Mom nodded in agreement.

Officer Peters sighed. "What kind of car did Mrs. Linkletter use?"

Uh oh. "I don't know different car types, but it was big. Like an SUV, maybe."

She scribbled something in her notebook. "What type of SUV? What colour? Did you see the logo?"

"No, I don't think so. I don't know cars. It was dark, though. Maybe black?"[3]

She took a sip of water and met my eyes, not my mother's. "Edan. Are you certain you saw this?"

"Um, yeah. That's why I called you, right?" My voice climbed into falsetto range.

"You're not trying to get attention by 'investigating' your principal? It's a serious offence to make up stories. It makes the police look for things like black SUV's and waste their time instead of focusing on the real perpetrators."

My mouth hung open for a long second before I clicked it closed.

Mom said, "It's not like Edan to make up stories."

"I understand that, Ms. Sze. I still have to ask questions." Officer Peters tapped the notepad with the end of the pen. "Edan, what are the chances you'd find that barrel and then, four days later, remember that you happened to see your principal on her last night?"

"We all saw her at school on Thursday," I said, stung. "I just happened to walk around that night. I saw someone who looked like her, wearing a dress and getting into a car."

"A car that wasn't hers."

"Right, she drives a silver car with lots of butterflies and flower stickers."

"So it might not be Mrs. Linkletter you saw at all."

I squeezed my eyes shut. "I know that."

"Yet you reached out to the private number I gave you."

"Because I want to—I'm trying to help you!" I bit back the fact that I might become a cop. At this rate, I'd change my mind.

She raised her eyebrows. "Yes, I know. I spoke to Garrett Smith."

Crap crap crap. "Yes, ma'am. I mean, yes, Officer."

"He told me you want to become a police officer. A detective."

"I'm thinking about it, Officer." *Thanks a billion, Garrett.*

She gave me a brief smile. "We appreciate young people and their enthusiasm. After all, you are the future."

I smiled back painfully, waiting for the "but."

"But sometimes it makes kids overexcited. They think that they see things they don't. They call us to tell us about it."[4]

I'm not doing that! I screamed silently to myself. *Why did you call me if you thought I was so useless?*

This interview seemed to take twice as long because Officer Peters grilled me about the time, where I walked, what else did I see, was I sure. By the time I signed a paper with all those details, I couldn't wait to disappear.

As she held the door open to the main hallway, Officer Peters said, "We appreciate you reaching out, Edan. We're looking for the truth, the whole truth, and nothing but the truth." She spoke loud enough that a passing officer paused to check us out.

I nodded mutely. I could not wait to get back to my friends, or just plain escape this place.

Officer Peters patted me on the shoulder. "Just keep it in mind."

I fumbled out a "Thank you," and ducked out the door, which clicked shut behind me.

14

I hustled toward Alta Drive, imagining the police watching my every step. Mom had offered to come with me, but it meant missing work that she'd have to make up later.

Finally out of sight, I checked my messages and answered Barstow and Callie with scared emojis 😨😵😱.

Callie dropped a bunch of sad faces in return.

You in?

I figured she meant hypnosis. I stopped to think about it outside a dim sum restaurant that smelled like steam and shrimp.

Finally, I sent Callie the thumbs up.

Barstow: *My house. Control room.*

I couldn't help grinning as I made my way over. Although Barstow's parents are cool, they make us leave the door open if we go in his bedroom. Parents are paranoid, what can I say.

Luckily, they don't apply the same rules to his basement "control room," where he keeps one of his computers (yeah, one of them. Jealous). The whole bottom floor is open concept, which means no doors except to the bathroom. You can run circles around the entire basement, which we used to do all the time as kids.[1]

After I joined them, Barstow closed and locked the main door to the basement. If his parents came, we'd pretend it had locked by accident. Easy peasy.

I dropped onto the couch that faces the TV, usually one of my favorite spaces. Barstow brought us some pop and chips to lighten the mood, but my throat had locked up, and Callie avoids junk food.

"Let's try and relax first," said Callie, although I could see the whites around her eyes. "Do you have any questions?"

Only about a million. I started with the easy one. "What will this feel like?"

"I don't know," she admitted, "but the people they interviewed afterward said they felt relaxed, almost like they were meditating or had gone to sleep."

I'd seen that too. I rubbed the leather arm of the couch, willing myself to relax. "What if I change my mind?"

"You can come out any time you get scared. You can make your own safe word, or a safe gesture."

Barstow nodded. "Usually, you rub your nose when you're worried. We could use that."

"I do?"

He grinned at me, and I realized why I never won when we played poker. Mr. Carver had taught us one day, and the three of us had tried it a few more times after school before I got sick of losing a bit to Callie and mostly to Barstow.[2]

"Okay, that sounds good. I guess." I swallowed hard.

Callie held up her hand. "I learned that it's better not to snap out of it with a clap or bang. I should gradually draw you out, like saying, 'I'll count down from five, and when I get to one, you'll re-alert and feel fresh.' So if you rub your nose, I'll do that. But please don't just rub your nose for fun."

I shook my head. "I didn't even know I rubbed my nose. How can I stop myself?"

"Don't," said Barstow. "You do it more when you're upset. I think we're safe to use it as a signal."

"Okay." My friends knew me better than I knew myself sometimes.

Callie cleared her throat. "I'll count you down and you can stop any time. Barstow is serious about this too."

I knew he was. I gave both of them a tight smile. "Okay. Let's do this."

15

Callie held both my hands in hers and told me to relax, like she was soothing a kitten.

I almost laughed until I thought of Mrs. L. I buttoned my mouth and squeezed my eyes shut, willing it to work. *This is Callie, one of your best friends in the world. She'd never hurt you on purpose. Let go.*

"Let go," said Callie at the same time.

Images started flashing in my mind.

You know when you're falling asleep and random things pop into your head that make no sense?[1]

First, dream-me left our apartment, but when Mr. Villalobos's door flew open, a wolf dog jumped out of his apartment, snarling.[2]

I stretched out my hand to pet it, and it closed its eyes. When my fingers sank into its thick fur, I seemed to leap straight into my own real memory of Thursday night.

I strolled up Barstow's street. A faint breeze blew my hair, so I tucked it behind my ears. The air smelled like motor oil with a whiff of the desert marigolds that spring up along the roads.

Car doors slammed. I slowed down, my eyes fixed on the crowd ahead. I recognized our Spanish teacher, Ms. Lopez, and Vernon's dad, both talking to Alicia's mom.

A Mini Cooper puttered off, chased by three more cars. One passed me, and I peered in the windshield. Mr. Eisen stared straight ahead, but I recognized his glasses and bald head.

As I drew closer, I focused on the woman talking to Mrs. Ness. She fiddled with her chunky bead necklace, and I recognized Ms. Garcia, Stephanie's mom, who helped with the yearbook.

But where was Mrs. Linkletter?

I searched for her stocky figure. Wait. A block ahead, her wavy brown and grey hair and purple dress glinted under the streetlight. She stood on the sidewalk, talking to someone in a dark vehicle.

Mrs. L? I couldn't tell from this distance. I started running, or tried to. My legs dragged like running through water.

"Mrs. L? Is that you?" I yelled, but she didn't turn.

I should get the license plate, I remembered, and darted into the street for a better view.

Definitely a Nevada plate. I read it out loud, but then I remembered the most important part, saving Mrs. L!

She climbed into the passenger seat, slamming the vehicle door after her.

I jogged after the SUV, cursing my lead legs. "Wait! Stop!"

The SUV took off, leaving a trail of exhaust up my nose.

16

Callie's voice floated by. "Is she okay?"

"Not really," said Barstow. "Let me see if I can find— hey. You see this? A guy in Canada did a mass hypnosis at a school, leaving a bunch of girls in a trance. One was stuck for five hours!"

"OMG, it says you shouldn't hypnotize anyone under fourteen."[1]

"Don't panic. There has to be a professional hypnotist who can—"

I dragged the words out of my throat. "... M'okay."

"Edan!" Callie shrieked.

I coughed. "My throat." More coughing.

Callie handed me a glass of water to sip. Barstow touched my shoulder, which was a massive deal for him.

I bit back another cough. "Did I—?"

"You read out the license plate," said Barstow. He showed it to me on a piece of paper.

"You look freaked out."

"You yelled about your legs."

"They didn't move right."

Barstow nodded. "You can't move any faster than when you were living it, right? You're trying to run under hypnosis, but you were walking in real life."

Callie frowned. "I don't know if that's a rule. I'd have to look it up."

"We don't care about what anybody else can do. Just Edan." Barstow sounded so fierce, I smiled at him. He frowned and turned away to fiddle with a paper clip on his desk.

I nodded and rasped, "The license plate?"

Barstow frowned, showing me the piece of paper. "You want to send it to the police?"

I shrugged. They hadn't seemed overwhelmed with gratitude for my tips.

Callie touched my arm. "This is a big one. I bet they'll want to know the license plate. It'll lead them right to whoever-it-is's door!"

I shook my head. They'd ask why I remembered the plate. Hypnosis by another teenager via YouTube sounded super sketchy. Truthfully, I'd never do it again.

"But we can't let whoever this is get away with murder if we can help it," said Callie.

We all sat with that for a second. Then I touched her arm to let her know I agreed.

Barstow held up his finger. "What about a third option? I could use a third party database."

"What's that?" asked Callie.

"Well, you can access the DMV's information, but they usually ask you to do it in person, with a paper trail, and maybe they're only open during school hours. Even if we were willing to line up, I think Nevada locks down owner information, so we might not get anything useful."

"Like what?" said Callie.

Barstow spun around to bring up a webpage. "See? In Nevada, you can ask the DMV for your own driving record for a job with a ride share service. And you can look for info for abandoned vehicles. But in our state, Callie Yang can't come up and ask for Amy Sze's driver info. It's a privacy thing. Only law enforcement and insurance companies get a free pass."[2]

I shook my head. Too bad that was useless for us.

Barstow's eyes sparkled behind his glasses. "But wait! A third party site takes your money and hands you the info. Private eyes do it all the time. All you have to do is pay a fee."

"Really? It's not, like, illegal?" asked Callie.

"Really. Here, see?" He switched to another website that promised us a fast, anonymous check. "All third parties care about is money. You pay, you're good."

I lifted my hand in the air. I still owed him for the Wheelzz to Red Rock.

Barstow reached for his own wallet. "I've got my Christmas and birthday money saved up."

I rushed to grab his hands and shook my head.

That stopped him. After a minute, he said, "I'm already in it knee deep, even after I clear out my cookies and web cache. It makes sense for me to pay the money."

Callie delicately cleared her throat. "I have a credit card for emergencies."

I held my arms up in an X. "No!"

"My parents let me pay them back if it's not an emergency, but they don't want me to get stuck somewhere without any way to get home."

Must be nice. But no, that wasn't fair. I searched my front pocket for my emergency $20.

"It's all right," said Callie, but I tunnelled into each pocket repeatedly, standing up for more room in my pants before I turned every pocket inside out.

"Hey. Has anyone seen my emergency $20?" I whispered, heart thumping.[3]

Barstow shook his head. "I never found mine in my desk, either."

I didn't want to ask Mom for another bill. Crap.

"Did you buy lunch with it one day and forget?" Callie asked.

I shook my head. I keep really careful track of my money. "The only thing I wanted to spend money on was a Civil War book, but it was more than $20." At least my voice worked better now. "I showed the site to Mr. Carver, and he said not to worry, he'd check the school budget."

Barstow scratched his chin. "Maybe that's why me and Callie heard Mrs. Linkletter, Mr. Carver, and Mr. Eisen arguing about money last week in the hall."

"Really? What did they say?" I couldn't breathe right, either from losing the money, the hypnosis, or both.

Callie handed me my water. "Mrs. Linkletter said, 'There's no more money.' Mr. Carver told her, 'There's always more money.' Mr. Eisen said they should check the school accounts again. Then they went in the teacher's lounge, so we didn't hear anything else."

"I guess that's why he didn't get my Civil War book."

Callie half-hugged me. "Maybe your $20 is in your other pants. Anyway, this DMV report will be my birthday present for *you*. You can pull in your birthday favor early." She smiled at me.

All of us silently remembered how her birthday favor had gone.

"Thanks," I said finally. I didn't have one penny on me. What could I do?

Barstow changed the subject. "I already bought you a Civil War present. I found it on eBay and had it delivered to the school under your name."

"Thanks." Mr. Villalobos's new toaster got stolen from our apartment doorstop, and now everyone's worried about missing deliveries. But the Wheelzz money, plus the third party search, made me feel guilty about yet another present. "Nothing too expensive, right?"

He snorted. "Twenty bucks plus shipping. No one but a real Civil War buff would want this one. Seriously, not a high monetary value."

I grinned at him. "Deal. I bet me and Mr. Carver will love it." I turned to Callie. "And I could really use the license report too. You sure? They might trace it back to you through the credit card."

"Who cares? I went to the police station already. If they ask, I'll tell them that you thought you remembered the plate number but wanted to check."

I'd buy that. I glanced at Barstow, who nodded.

I took a deep breath. "Okay. Let's do it."

Barstow clicked through the website, which I noticed he'd loaded on a private browser. He knows how to cover his tracks. Callie entered the credit card info.

Now we waited for it to pop up the owner's name, which took forever.

Barstow held up his index finger like he was a teacher, meaning one minute. I rolled my eyes, and Callie laughed at both of us and pointed at the progress bar on the bottom of the screen. "It's coming."

"Okay." I closed my eyes and tried to meditate. Mrs. L had held meditation sessions in the auditorium once, to try and promote world peace. We'd giggled then. I felt bad about that now. I closed my eyes and slowed down my breathing, trying to inhale in. Out. In. Out.

"Oh," said Barstow, and my eyes flew open and read the owner's name in the middle of the screen.

LINKLETTER, ALOYSIUS A

17

"Al—" I couldn't even pronounce that first name. "Linkletter. That doesn't help us at all, does it?"

"No, it's good news," said Callie. "You remembered the plate number. Right on!" She held out her fist for a bump.

I bumped it, although I nearly missed before I connected.

"Can we look up how he's related to Mrs. Linkletter?" Callie nosed the computer mouse around.

"Sure." Barstow took over the keyboard. "Got it. Her husband." He brought up a picture of the two of them that had made it into the school yearbook a few years ago.

"Her *husband* killed her?" asked Callie, stepping back from the monitor.

"Well, he owns the car that picked her up." Barstow wheeled around in his chair to check my face. "We'll let the police figure that out."

I sighed. "After we tell Officer Peters."

"They might already know." Barstow rubbed his nose. "They should have checked him out. That's the number one suspect in most cases, right? The husband."

Callie cleared her throat. "I think you should say partner now."

I felt like throwing something, like a dodgeball or a fit. "Either way, now I have to talk to the police about this. Unless it could be an anonymous tip?"

Callie jumped to her feet and punched the air. "They have a hotline. Remember, they set one up. Good one!"

Barstow swivelled his seat side to side. "That's a good idea. Call from a pay phone, though."

I gave him the thumbs up sign for ultimate anonymity.

Callie started to pace around Barstow's desk, making semi circles around us. "Do you want the reward? They must need a way of identifying you to give you the money."

Money. Mom and I could really use that. Not to mention presents for my friends, or just plain repaying them.[1] Then I told myself to forget it. It wasn't worth the hassle. I had two best friends and a mom who always looked after me. I couldn't ask for anything more.

"I'll worry about that later," I said.

Callie tipped her head to the side, her dark hair flowing over her shoulder. "Did anyone else report her getting into that car? If not, Officer Peters might figure out it's you."

I held my breath, then sighed. "Yeah, she probably will. But I still have to tell them, and the hotline will let me do it without an interrogation."

"Or them telling you you're an overexcited little kid," Barstow muttered, picking up a Rubik's cube to scramble it.

I nodded at him. "Exactly."

Callie squeezed my hand. "I could call the hotline instead, if you want. I already gave my parents' credit card info."

"Really? You'd do that for me?"

Callie gulped, but she nodded.

I squeezed my eyes shut. "I would *so* appreciate it."

Callie took a deep breath and squared her shoulders like before a swim meet. "Done."

"You're the best." I hugged her and sniffed, trying not to get snot on her shoulder.

"I wish I could help more," said Barstow in a low voice.

"You've helped tons," I said, while Callie released me and yelped, "We couldn't do this without you."

"Avoiding the police holds me back from being a full team player,[2] but I did get more intel for you. Up to you if you want it or not."

"Why wouldn't I want intel? We're trying to solve this case."

Barstow glanced at Callie, then back at me. "It has nothing to do with this case. It's more like your family."

I blinked at him. "You found more about my father?"

"Got it in one."

"What did you find out?" I hadn't dug up much dirt on Edward Wong. Now that I thought about it, I'd probably distracted myself with Red Rock. For so many years, I'd yearned for my dad before mostly pushing him out of my mind.

Barstow clicked open a document onto his desktop. "Do you want to see it, or keep going with Mrs. L?"

I tiptoed toward the screen. Barstow stood to give me the chair.

Callie twisted her hands, but stayed in her seat.

"It's okay," I told her, gesturing at her to read over my shoulder. I didn't want to repeat it afterward anyway.

She moved beside me, and Barstow sat on the desk, both of them flanking me as I read.

18

My father, Edward Wong, lived in Hong Kong.

I exhaled in relief and screwed my eyes shut. I wanted my father alive and available if I chose to reach out, but not in my face. The other side of the planet worked for me. Also, it rhymed. Edward Wong in Hong Kong.

I memorized his address, even though I didn't know Hong Kong at all. "Just in case," I whispered. Seeing the words on the screen made him more real.

"I can send you everything." Barstow watched me from his perch on the desk. "You don't have to go through it in front of us."

"I want to." Now that I'd made even electronic contact with my dad's address, I wouldn't let it go. Callie touched my shoulder as I scrawled it onto a thick piece of paper with a fancy ink pen that Barstow handed me.

Edward Wong (Eddie?) had made quite a splash in the legal world. He'd joined a successful practice in Hong Kong before striking out on his own.

He'd also married a woman named Sarah and had two boys named Isaac and Liam, younger than me, of course.

"I bet they don't sleep on a pull-out couch," I muttered.[1]

"You want to keep going?" Callie looked worried.

"Sure. Looks like they also own a place in Vegas." That stabbed my heart harder than him having another family. Well, about as much. "You think they come here for vacations?"

Callie typed into her phone and played with her bottom lip. "I think they live here now. The Hong Kong law office doesn't list him anymore."

"Agreed." Barstow clicked on another window for me. "He's not part of the 'our team' page if you look him up. I wonder if he also had to escape Hong Kong because of the politics."

I blinked at Callie's screen before mapping out his Vegas address on the monitor. "If they moved here, they live in Green Valley. You think I could have passed my own dad in the street without knowing it?"

Callie and Barstow exchanged a look before he said, "I doubt it. You look a lot like him."

Callie elbowed him. "Barstow!"

"What? She hasn't even gotten to the pictures yet."[2]

The room seemed to blur. My breath caught in my throat.

"You don't have to look at them now. Or ever," Barstow added quickly, shutting the monitor off.

"No!" I grabbed his arm hard enough to leave red marks.

Barstow clicked the monitor back on with his free hand, and I stared at pictures of Edward, Sarah, Isaac, and Liam Wong until I cried.

19

"It's too much for her," Callie whispered. Her voice sounded like she orbited above me while I sat crumpled in the desk chair.

"She wanted to." Barstow crossed his arms, I noticed out of the corners of my blurry vision. I covered my eyes and rubbed my nose on my sleeve.

Callie hugged me from behind for a quick second, even though she got more of the chair than me. "Yes, but ... the whole thing with Mrs. L, and then her mom sprung her dad's info on her, and I hypnotized her, and we probably figured out who killed Mrs. L, but first you showed her dad's whole other family."

I could hear them, but I didn't care. I'd dropped off the cliff of shock into the valley of numb.[1]

"We need to get her home," said Callie.

"She's checked out. You don't think her mom will notice? And what about Garrett?"

Callie paused. "You think he's at her place?"

"He's there half the time."

"That's true. You don't like him?"

"You know I don't."

"Yeah, but I don't know why."

Barstow didn't answer for a long time. I almost turned to look at him, but my body felt locked up. Different from hypnosis, when I'd been weighed down. Now I couldn't move at all.

At least my ears worked.

"I don't trust him." Barstow checked the basement door before closing it again.

"He does put on a Mr. Nice Guy act," Callie agreed.

"More than that. I think he acts dumber than he is. And he watches us all the time, especially Edan."

"Why do you sleep over at her place, then?"

"I'm looking out for her. I don't want her to be alone with him."[2]

One mystery solved, but I didn't even twitch.

Callie stumbled over her words. "You—you think he'd hurt her?"

"It wouldn't surprise me."

I opened my mouth, then closed it. Let's face it. It wouldn't surprise me, either.

I loved my mom, not her taste in guys.

Although Garrett might be a cop, none of us trusted him.

20

Callie wrapped a blanket around me, surrounding me in soft microfleece. I wiped my eyes and smiled at her. Yep, I'd officially unfrozen.

A tea kettle whistled. Pretty soon, Barstow returned with a hot cup of tea and a box of tissues, both of which he placed on the desk in front of me. "Don't get tea in the keyboard, though."[1]

That was so much like him that I cracked a grin.

Callie asked softly, "You going to be okay?"

I took a sip of tea, which I don't normally drink, but this was an emergency. He'd added lots of sugar. I nodded and whispered, "Thanks. I didn't mean to ... fall apart."

"Are you kidding me? I would have dropped to the ground."

Total exaggeration. You can't break swim records lounging around like a delicate iris. But I grinned anyway.

"You were due," Barstow agreed. "You've been through more shocks than anyone."

I took a deep breath. "Well, I'm back."

"You never left," Callie agreed. "Now what should we do?"

They both stared at me, my two friends that I loved and trusted more than anything. Only my mom had cared for me longer. I would've missed my dad a lot more, and been more screwed up in general, without these two. That made me want to cry again.

Instead, I drank my tea and said, "Where can we find a pay phone?"[2]

Barstow crinkled his nose. "I remember seeing one at a gas station."

"Me too," said Callie, "but which one?"

"May I?" Barstow took over the computer again. It's faster than Wifi because of the Ethernet cable. Within seconds, he showed us a list of Vegas pay phones online. I started checking out the locations but realized we didn't have a lot of choices.

"I'll tell my dad that I need to buy some sports equipment near this one," Callie decided, holding up her phone's map. "He'll give me a ride down. But we can't all go. He might take me for a quick run at the end of the night, but not a whole expedition with the three EBC."

We agreed glumly. Mr. Yang would wonder why the three of us suddenly had to shop but ended up clustered in a phone booth, when we all had cell phones.

"It means you'll have to report the license plate alone," I said. "It feels wrong." We'd done everything as a team except police visits.

Callie pointed to my piece of paper with Edward's work and home address, phone numbers, and email. "Are you going to ... "

"I don't know," I admitted out loud. Should I contact him? Or leave him alone with his perfect family?

"Up to you." Barstow quickly changed the subject after my low-level freak out. "Is there anything else we can do about the Mrs. L case while you're working on the hotline?"

I took a few breaths and managed to switch gears. "Do you have anything on Al-whatever Linkletter?"

21

"He owns a construction company," Barstow tilted the monitor so we could all check the hits. "Pretty sure he's the only Aloysius in town, at least in the right age range."

"They have three adult kids." Callie pointed at a photo from their last wedding anniversary.

"I wonder how the kids and maybe grandkids are taking it," I said.

Barstow glanced at the screen, and I knew what he was thinking. We'd ruin those lives even more if Mr. Linkletter was the last person to see his wife alive.

"I'd rather know," said Callie, throwing her shoulders back. "Let me call my dad and see if I can get a ride to the pay phone."

I hugged her tightly.

"I'm not going to the moon." She laughed.

"I know." I didn't let go of her for another second anyway.

Barstow gave her a thumbs up sign when she left.[1]

I packed up my water bottle, and Barstow stared at his hands while he said, "You might end up liking Eddie."

I dropped my water bottle. "My father? Why shouldn't I rip him a new one? He left me and my mom. I'm the poorest kid in my class while he lives the high life in Green Valley and maybe in Hong Kong too."

"Not the poorest. And your mother didn't want him to know about you."

Mom did say that.

"She was afraid she'd lose you," Barstow said. "He had money and a law degree, or almost a degree, and she was a penniless actress."[2]

I clicked back to what my mom said, which I'd repeated back to my friends that night, and closed my eyes. *If he'd known about you, he might have tried to take you away from me.* "Oh, crap."

"Right. And I get why she was scared. If it went to court, who would have won? The lawyer or the actress with no money?"

"No contest. Okay, so I can't blame him for not reaching out when he didn't know I existed." I paused. "Still, it doesn't mean I *can't* contact him, especially since you handed me all his info. It just means ... "

"He won't know what hit him. And your mom won't want to lose custody." Barstow sighed. After a second, though, he snapped his fingers. "Hold up. I don't know that he'd fight over you because he already has two boys, plus I think he'd be liable for child support. You and your mom wouldn't be poor anymore!"

Weird weird weird weird weird.

"I don't know how Garrett would react either," I said slowly, choosing not to think about money, for the second time tonight. "He liked the idea of me chasing down my bio dad more than me investigating the Red Rock killer. But I bet he didn't expect you to turn this all up in 24 hours. How would Garrett react to a new man in our lives? Or even one who was here a long time ago?"

"Dunno," said Barstow. He got up and shifted his weight from foot to foot.

"Stardew?" I suggested.

"Always."

I used his upstairs computer to unwind in Stardew Valley. I planted and picked a satisfying number of blueberries on our virtual farm and we made it to level 99 in the mines before Callie called.

22

I ran downstairs so Callie could tell both of us together in real time. She didn't want to text about something like this.

"How'd it go?" I asked.

"Okay, I guess. I made it to the phone booth and left a message, that's all."

"Good job," said Barstow.

"Plus my dad overheard me saying Mr. Linkletter's name."

I sucked in my breath. "What?"

Barstow muttered a few choice words.

"He was totally cool with it. He said, 'Oh, you remember Mr. Linkletter from when you were in first grade?' And then I realized, I did!"

"You did?"

"Where? When?" Barstow snapped at the same time.

"He coached me in swimming when I was six. He wasn't very good, and he asked us to call him Al, so I forgot about him until now."

"How was he?" I asked.

"Kind of boring. He made us do the drills over and over again at the Y, and he wouldn't let me dive in the deep end, even though I knew how to already."

I frowned. "That sounds familiar. Maybe I had him too."

Barstow brought up Aloysius Linkletter's picture through an images search narrowed to location and swimming teachers.

I pointed to one close-up and nodded. "There was a guy named Al. He kept telling me to use my arms more.[1] I think that's part of the reason I quit swimming."

"I had him too. I thought he was okay," said Barstow. "But you know what this means, right?"

"No," Callie and I chorused.

"We could talk to him. If we wanted to."

"Nooooooooooo!" Callie and I said, and then we laughed and said "Jinx." But we had so many real jinxes, we stopped laughing.

"Hear me out. We don't have to meet him at Red Rock or anything crazy like that. We could go to the Linkletter house during the daytime and bring him muffins. We'd stay on the porch, say, 'Hello, you used to teach us swimming. Mrs. L was our principal. Sorry for your loss.'"

He said the last bit like he'd had practice. Not me. I'd never been to a funeral.

Callie asked, "But what good would that do?"

"Edan could check out his vehicle. Really casual. See if it looks like a black SUV with the right license plate. And you're good at talking to grown ups."

"I am not!" Callie exclaimed. We all laughed, even her, so she shot back, "What about you, Barstow? It was your PTA meeting, or at least your mom's. It would be a lot more natural if you said hi to 'Al.' So you'll step up and chat him up with muffins, or you want me to do it?"

"Barstow did a ton of background research," I said. "Way better than what I could do. Let's not fight."

Callie simmered down. She hates fighting too. "Sorry. That was amazing info on Mr. Wong. Can you find anything else on Mr. Linkletter? Like what does he do again?"

"He owns that construction company."

"So he's good with his hands," I said.

"Well, he's the owner, so not necessarily," said Barstow. "But usually they work their way up."

"He'd have access to saws and drills and barrels," Callie said. "And, like, excavators to hide the body!"

I gasped.

Barstow made a face. "Nah. Then he'd go to his construction site instead of Red Rock."

"He might not have wanted the body so close to his work. And he was the last person to see his wife alive, that we know of," I said. "This all means we should stay as far away from him as possible. Let the police see that he owns the car, and bam. They can question him all they want!"[2]

23

We argued over it until Callie said, "I'm hungry. Let's make muffins, anyway."

Barstow's mom ended up driving us over to my little apartment after supper, supposedly so we could study biology.

"It's cozy at your place," said Callie. "And you have at least three old bananas."

My mom doesn't like throwing anything out, so we found six old, frozen bananas in the freezer. While we gently zapped those to defrost them, metal measuring spoons tinkled together as Barstow measured out the flour.[1]

"Let's double the recipe so we can eat some too," I said, and we all agreed.

As Callie cleared the counter, she paused at the toaster oven. "What's a pink book doing here?"

"Oh, my mom's diary. She likes to hide it." I plucked it from behind the toaster oven.

"But she shouldn't put it behind the toaster. It's a fire hazard," Callie said.[2]

"Garrett might have cleaned it away, or she shoved it there because he was coming over. He's a neat freak."

"I guess."

I caught the look on Barstow's face when we talked about Garrett. No, I hadn't hallucinated him saying that he didn't trust my mother's boyfriend.

I tossed Mom's diary in the cupboard above the stove, which we all agreed was not a fire hazard.

"I just need to go to the bathroom first." Callie hopped toward it.

"Sure, just don't bang on the toilet, okay? Mr. Villalobos goes nuts. He said the next time, he'll call the cops."

Callie had already flicked on the bathroom's light switch. "Do you really think Mr. Villalobos would call the cops? For what?"

"For disturbing the peace."

"And who would bang on a toilet?"

I made a face. "Mom dropped her conditioner the other day."

Callie rolled her eyes. "Who doesn't?"

"I guess she's in the bathroom a lot. We don't even have a bathtub, so she soaks her feet in a bucket with bath salts."

We giggled over that. Well, Callie and I did while Barstow mashed up the bananas.

Soon we feasted on piping hot banana muffins, which put me in such a good mood that I said, "I changed my mind. Let's do it."

"Do what?" demanded Barstow.

"Talk to Mr. Linkletter. We've got the world's best banana muffins, and he can't do anything to us in public."

"What if he waited so he could do something to us later?" Barstow wanted to know.

"We'll dress up and give fake names. He won't remember us from when we were six."

"Says you," said Barstow.

I rummaged on my phone for pictures of Barstow in first grade. "You seriously think you still look like this?"

He snorted.

"I bet we could dig up their address." I unlocked my phone. "Hey, we don't even have to go to their house. They're having a memorial service at the funeral home tomorrow at noon!"

Barstow shook his head. "School."

"No, here's a thing from the school letting us go if we want. Mr. Eisen said it's so that we can 'process the trauma.' Best time to talk to Mr. Linkletter!"

"You still want me to ask him?" Barstow started scratching muffin crumbs off his liner, not meeting my eyes.

I sipped some milk. "Nah, I don't mind. I'll tell Mr. L that my mom's in the PTA. He won't know the difference." I paused. "You have Asian moms in the PTA, right?"

"Sure." Callie popped her head back in from where she'd started washing dishes. "I've seen Ms. Wang, Mrs. Kim, Ms. Suzuki, Mrs. Lee, the other Mrs. Wang—"

"I'll take Wang," I decided. "It's a common name, plus there's more than one already. That'll work." It was also the closest to my father's name. What if I accidentally ended up pretending to be my father's daughter in front of a potential murderer? My heart fluttered, but I refused to let fear stop me. "Let's do this."

24

I walked into the funeral home with a plateful of banana muffins. I'd never seen so many of my classmates in black at once. It was kind of eerie. I recognized at least ten different kids standing around uncomfortably.

My hands sweated and I felt sick, partly because Callie and Barstow and me had split apart. I hated being alone, but we all agreed that three kids alone together, especially two Asian girls and a Black boy, was way more noticeable than us separated.

Callie had come early with her mom. Barstow had arrived second with his friend Trudeau (I swear they bonded over weird names, but whatever works). Now me, walking in with Ava, Alicia Ramirez, and another classmate. I lost them when I hung back to unwrap the muffins. No one else had brought food, and Alicia had said, "What are those, E-Z?"[1]

I'd never been inside a funeral home before. It looked like a fancy beige building with a big black and white sign on the outside. On the inside, it looked like a house with lots of rooms and a high ceiling. Grey carpet, I think to make it more quiet, while they piped some instrumental music through their sound system.

"You Are My Sunshine" made me bite the inside of my cheek. My mom likes that song and used to sing it to me when I was a baby.

I thought I recognized Callie's mom's handwriting in the guest book, even as I pretended not to look. So much for anonymity.

A tall man with a big gut wearing a fancy suit said, "For Mrs. Linkletter?"

I nodded.

He handed me a booklet and nodded at my muffins. "Sorry for your loss. Would you like me to take those?"

I hesitated. "Will you give them to Mr. Linkletter and tell them they're from Forester Middle School?"

"Of course."

I didn't want to keep hanging on to food that no one else had, but it seemed like we'd done the work for nothing when he disappeared with the muffins.

The booklet picture of Mrs. L looked a lot younger. I flipped through it, avoiding the eyes of two women coming toward me on the opposite side of the hall.

"... a disgrace," said one of them.

"We can take comfort in each other. So many people are coming that the family asked some to participate online instead of coming in person."

"Well, it is lovely that so many people loved Gretel. Did you see all the little students?"

Ha. Little. Barstow was almost as tall as his mom, although as skinny as a pipe. I haven't hit a big growth spurt yet, though. I kept my head turned away, staring at a print of a lily. I could see both women reflected in the glass. They were short and pudgy with greying hair.

"Some came because of what happened to her," said the one in a dress with colors swirled together, black mixed with green, blue, and even yellow.

"You can't blame them. Even for Las Vegas, this is shocking. Someone shot her and abandoned her in that barrel."[2]

I held my breath. Someone shot her? How would these women know? Could one of them work for the police?

"Yes. Shot twice. At least we know that she didn't suffer."

"She could have suffered beforehand, you know."

I sucked in my breath.

"No, the experts thought she'd died within minutes. I have my sources, Francine."

"I'm sure you do, Farah."

Farah and Francine. What a funny pair. I pretended to retie my shoelace.

"Listen to us talk. We should find Al and the rest of his family."

"Absolutely. But first, I really must find the restroom."

I waited for them to move off first, and then I continued down the hallway.

I should have known I'd find more information by coming to the memorial service. The detectives always go to funerals in books and movies. I couldn't wait to tell Barstow and Callie.

"Do you need a moment, Dad?" asked another voice, and I noticed a man leading an even older man using a cane. I turned my head to get a better look.

Mr. Linkletter! I recognized the older man's nose, even though the rest of him seemed to have hunched and shrunk compared to what I remembered over seven years ago. His wrists stuck out of his suit jacket.

Could he really have killed his wife? I guess it doesn't take much to pull a trigger, but how would he have gotten her in a barrel?

Unless he was playing up the angle of the grieving old widower? Or he had help?

Morbid thoughts, my mom would say. *Police officer thoughts*, I'd tell her. I kept an eye on the Linkletters through my daffodil print's reflection.

"You can't blame yourself, Dad. You did everything you could," said the son.

Mr. L muttered something in return.

His son answered, "You picked her up from that meeting after she had car trouble. You were ready to bring her home. It's not your fault that she wanted to fix things and meet with that lawyer, whatever his name is."

Mr. Linkletter mumbled again.

My skin prickled even before the son said, "Yeah, that's right. He better not show his face here, I'll tell you that. I'll check if the police have got anything on Edward Wong."

25

Edward Wong.
　　My father.
　　My father, the lawyer.
No. Way.
But how many lawyers were named Edward Wong in Las Vegas?

I stumbled toward a water fountain and drank from it, almost gulping like a dog. Then I pulled out my phone and started to search.

I found 25 local records of Edward Wong, but only one who had a license to practice law in Nevada with an office address matching the one that Barstow had given me.

My father. I hadn't even found him yet. Utter rock bottom way to meet your father. *Hello, Daddy. You've never seen me before, but did you kill Mrs. Linkletter?*

I hurried to the bathroom and splashed water on my face, trying not to soak the multiple boxes of tissues lined up along the mirrors.

"Are you okay, dear?" asked the swirly dress woman, Felicity or Farah or whatever.

I tried to smile at her.

"Oh, you poor thing. How shocking it must be for you and your classmates. You probably go to Forester Middle School, isn't that right?"

Uh oh. This woman knew too much, or acted like she did. I didn't want to tell her anything. So I started blinking and rubbing my eyes like I might cry.

"You darling. I can tell that you must be one of her little Foresters." She started to hug me while I stiffened.

Ugh. Did cops hug you? That seemed over the top. She smelled like old perfume, and I could see the wrinkles in her neck, close up. She wore dangly earrings with little skulls on them.[1]

"Do you want me to bring you to see your parents? You shouldn't be alone when you're so upset."

Darn. I'd overdone my poor child act. I couldn't tell her I'd come alone. She might not let a technically 13-year-old escape on her own.

"I'll call my sister," I sniffed, holding up my phone.[2]

"I'll wait for you while you call. Don't you worry. I have a lot of tissues if you need one."

"Thanks." I glanced at the solid row of tissue boxes near the mirrors.

"Mine are better. You don't want to touch things that a thousand strangers have handled." She pulled out a little packet of tissues, forcing me to take one. "Now call that sister of yours."

I quickly dialled Callie. Luckily, she picked up right away.

"Hey, it's me," I said, striving for a brave orphan tone. "I'm in the bathroom and kind of a mess. A lady is helping me call my sister."

Callie got it right away. She recognized my number and voice and knew that I had no sister but that she should pretend to be one. "I'll come find you. You sit tight."

Five minutes later, Callie and her mom and I hurried out of the bathroom, waving 'bye to the woman who knew too much.

26

"Don't worry," said Mrs. Yang. "Everyone's upset about Mrs. L."

I was upset, but not the way she thought. Barstow took one look at my face and agreed to a ride to the Yang's house.

I could hardly wait until the three of us got to Callie's room and locked the door. Then I spilled the tea, stumbling over my words. I was too shook.

"They said Mrs. Linkletter went to see a lawyer named Edward Wong *after* the PTA meeting."

Callie gasped.

"Your *father* was the last person to see Mrs. L alive?" Barstow's mouth twisted like he didn't know whether to believe me or not.

"That's what the Linkletters are saying!"

"It doesn't mean it's true," Barstow assured me.[1]

"But what if it is?" I started to pace. Not much room. I managed to navigate between and around Callie's enormous bed, her dresser, her comfy chair, and her desk.

"Are you going to tell the police about that?" Callie wanted to know.

"No. The son added something about hoping the police caught him, so they must already know."

"I wonder if Mr. Linkletter wanted to get himself off the hook when the police questioned him," said Callie.

"But that's just it," said Barstow. "We don't have proof yet that your dad shot Mrs. L, only that her husband and son say she had an appointment with him. What kind of lawyers take appointments after 5 p.m.?"

"Criminal lawyers," I said softly. "There are no tax or corporate emergencies." I couldn't remember what kind of law he practiced, but it wasn't criminal. I would've remembered that.

"Maybe he's a criminal lawyer, too," Callie put in after a long silence. "He's been away a long time. He could do two types of law instead of one!"

"In Hong Kong?" I asked. That was already a big deal. I couldn't imagine practicing two types of law in two different languages, English and Cantonese. Three if he worked in Mandarin.

"Maybe they need more criminal lawyers around the world," Callie insisted, but we all thought that sounded iffy. Barstow wouldn't even meet my eyes.

"Guess we need to find my dad after all," I said in a hollow voice. "In case he's the Red Rock Killer."[2]

"If he's the Red Rock Killer, you need to stay away!" Barstow half-yelled at me. "If he calls you, if he texts you, don't answer."

"Even if I don't talk to him, my mom might. I wonder if that's why she finally told me. Not only to distract me, but because my dad was in town. Maybe Garrett got a clue through the police department."

"Stay away," Barstow repeated.

I didn't answer. My dad had returned to Las Vegas and might be the Red Rock Killer.

I needed to protect my mother from him.

If my friends refused, I'd search for Edward Wong myself.

"Mom, do you want to go for a walk? Just us?" I set my cup in the sink and pasted my most winning smile on my face, even though my temples pounded. I really did feel like crying after that funeral home shock and the long wait for Mom's key in the lock.

Mom glanced up from her phone. She'd stretched her legs out on the couch that would turn into my bed. "Hmm? Oh, honey, Garrett wants to take me out tonight. We've been working so hard."

"I miss you." I tried to widen my eyes like an anime character, but I bumped my hip into the kitchen cupboard and probably looked like a clumsy Muppet. "Didn't you say 'sisters before misters'?"

Well, she wasn't my sister. How about ... daughter before slaughter?[1]

She grinned and crossed over to the sink to ruffle my hair. "You miss me enough to go for a walk?"

I swatted her hand away. "I walk. In the mornings and after it cools down in the evenings."

"Not since ... " She stopped. She didn't want to bring up the Red Rock Killer.

Neither did I. Especially not right now, but like Mom said, needs must. "Don't you want some fresh air?" Mom always asked me that, so I turned it back on her.

Mom stuck her tongue out at me, which used to be my favorite move, so I laughed until she added, "Should we invite Garrett?"

My eyes popped. *No no no no no no no.* "I need some girl time."

Mom hugged me. "Good idea. I know it's especially important in puberty."

"Mom, gross!"

She grinned. "Sorry, Edan. I'll tell Garrett to come in an hour. Is that enough time? Boy, you look serious."

"It's important." My voice shook a little. I hoped she didn't notice.

"Okay. Let me clean up." She replaced her pen in our pencil holder in the kitchen and ported her diary into her room. (I'd remembered to stick the diary back behind the toaster, but moved the toaster away from the outlet, to decrease the chance of fire. 'Cause the only thing worse than having a tiny one bedroom apartment is *not* having a tiny one bedroom apartment.)

I picked a plain black shirt and shorts. I heard her opening and closing some drawers, and then Mom emerged in an oversized blue

T-shirt advertising mutual funds and her stretchy black shorts that show an underwear line.

"Uh, ready to go?" I'm no fashion plate, but it's not like I try to look bad in public. Not something to fight about today, though. "Thanks, Mom."

She kissed my cheek. "I miss our girl time."

"Me too." Mostly I hang out with Callie and Barstow now, but it felt good to follow her down the stairs.

"What do you want to talk about?" Her voice echoed down the stairwell.

"I'll tell you outside." Probably safer inside, but I found it easier to talk sometimes without staring her face to face.

For once, maybe because she was with me, Mr. Villalobos didn't chase us out.

"I hope you've given up on your ... summer plans," she said, holding the door open for me.

I scooted out the door. The heat hit me, even though it was 7:40 p.m. and I'd lived in Vegas all my life. "I want to talk to you about what I found. The information that I have now."

Her sneakers slapped on the sidewalk. She liked to walk fast, so I caught up with her, and she grinned and slowed down. "I'm all ears."

I waited for a group of tattooed motorcyclers to pass us so I didn't have to shout over their engines. "He's here."

"Who?" Her eyebrows jumped.

"Edward Wong." I couldn't bring myself to say "my father."

Her lips shaped an O, and she half-whistled under her breath. "Okay. You found him already?"

"I have an address. I haven't contacted him yet." I tried to think of the best way to put it and then gave up. "But I have reason to believe that he might have been the last person to see Mrs. L alive."

She stopped walking in front of a convenience store. It took her a minute to process this, while the OPEN sign flashed red on her face and a Slushie ad hung over us.

I waited, watching her face flicker through shock, denial, and anger. "Edan. I know you have a big imagination—"

"It's not my imagination, Mom! I went to the memorial today, and the Linkletters were talking about it."

"What did they say?"

I picked my words out. "Mr. L picked her up from the PTA meeting at Barstow's house, but she had to go for a meeting with her lawyer, who's named Edward Wong."

Mom shook her head. "That's impossible. Your dad would never meet anyone in the evening. He'd have a secretary book an appointment between 9 and 5. Maybe 9 to 4."

"I'm telling you what I heard, Mom."

She raised her eyebrows. "They have to be mistaken."

"Do you want to call Mr. Linkletter and ask him? He and his son said she met with Edward Wong. I heard them."

"There has to be another Edward Wong. Even if your dad were back in the country, he's a lawyer. He doesn't meet anyone at night."

I swallowed. "He's not *supposed* to meet anyone at night."[2]

She did a 180 back toward our apartment, walking even faster now. I had to run to catch up. "They must have mixed up the name, or you heard wrong, or it's a different Edward Wong."

"Mom, there aren't any other lawyers in Las Vegas named Edward Wong."

She turned on me fiercely. "Your father did. Not. Kill. Mrs. Linkletter."

A woman walking her dog walked into the road to avoid Mom's intensity. The dog wagged its tail uncertainly.

"I don't want it to be true either, Mom. I'm only telling you what I heard. If you called, you could ask Mr. Linkletter, or his son—"

"Leave this to the police, Edan! How many times do I have to tell you?" She punched in the building code without meeting my eyes. "You dream big, but this is too much. No more Red Rock for you. I forbid you to go out or to do any more 'investigation.' Is that clear?"

28

Mom wouldn't speak to me when we got home except to confiscate my phone. She powered it down and stuck it in her purse, meaning I had zero access.

I lay down on the couch and covered my head with my pillow so I wouldn't have to watch.

Still, I could hear her calling Garrett. "Edan is grounded," she told him. "I'll have to stay in tonight. You want to come over?"

Please, no. I rolled on my side, one ear against the sofa cushions, one against the pillow, willing him to veto it. *You're busy, you don't like our messy apartment ...* [1]

"Great. You don't have to bring anything except yourself." She laughed next. "Well. If you insist."

Uh oh. I made a mental note to wear my headphones if they headed into the bedroom. Gross.

"Yes. See you then, big guy." She cracked a smile, and I wished I could talk to Barstow and Callie, but I'd been cut off. *You can live without this phone for 24 hours, Edan. You should meditate and read and ground yourself in the real world instead of ... other things.*

I groaned. What if I had to research something for school? Or look up the Civil War?

I whacked my pillow against the armrest a few times, just to make a noise that wasn't screaming.

My mom clucked her tongue. "Don't be so dramatic. You can always use the landline." She pointed at the black plastic phone mounted on the wall between the kitchen and the living room.

I couldn't even remember the last time I'd touched that phone. We kept the landline for emergencies. [2] Working for the police, Mom believed in backup plans, even if she made a face every time she had to pay the extra bill.

"Thanks," I muttered. Maybe if she got distracted enough by Garrett, I could update either Barstow or Callie through the landline.

Maybe.

Mom pointed at the dishes in the sink, and I turned on the hot water, feeling like Cinderella. I needed some cute mouse friends to help me, though.

"Thank you, Edan." She paused with her lipstick her hand. "I know you mean well. You're a bright girl with a big heart. Take the next 24 hours to recenter yourself, okay?"

"Okay," I muttered, even though I wanted to ask, *What does recentering even mean?*

Garrett's key slid into the lock. I sat on my couch bed, wishing for a bedroom with a door to lock behind me, or a quick escape to Barstow's.

But grounded Edan was a visible Edan, so I picked up a Robin Hobb book and held it in front of me while I waved at him.

Garrett stopped kissing my mom, glancing over her head to say, "Edan, I want to talk to you."

I tensed, almost ripping the cover of the book. "Hi, Garrett."

He walked into the apartment, his shoes clacking on the floor. My mom asked every other person to remove their shoes. We even have a sign near the door. But Garrett always wore his shoes inside.

My toes curled inside my socks. I tried to smile anyway.

"Your mother tells me you've gotten too deep into this case."

I glanced at my mother. I'd made her swear not to tell Garrett about my bio dad possibly seeing Mrs. Linkletter the night that she'd died. Mom had promised to keep quiet if at all possible. *It's all speculation, Edan. Why would I tell Garrett that on our date night?*

Mom shook her head at me, meaning that she hadn't told him about Edward.

I relaxed slightly, but I watched Garrett, who sat beside me, spreading his legs apart to take up more room like that subway meme about guys who "manspread."

I shot Mom a help-me look.

She held up her hand: *hear him out.*

I rolled my eyes inside and held my book. If nothing else, I could set the book down between us, making a barrier.

"Now, I admire your tenacity." Garrett looked pleased with himself for using a vocabulary word. "You're a firecracker like your mother. But Red Rock is for experts. You need to move on."

Move on? It hadn't even been a week since we found Mrs. L. I tried to channel how Callie would tell him that, but couldn't think with Garrett sitting too close. "Huh."

"You may well become an excellent policewoman in the next ten years. You can apply to the academy. We're always looking for diversity hires."

I nearly stuck my tongue out at him.

"Or whatever it's called by then. You know what I mean. But Red Rock is the big leagues. You and Callie did your part by pointing out the barrel. Now it's our job to look after it. You hear me?"

"Yeah." Sure I heard him. I couldn't close my ears. I gave a quick nod.

"Now, you probably feel anxious about your principal. That's normal. You should talk to your school counsellors about that. But sleep well tonight knowing that we've made significant progress in this case. We should make an announcement soon." He winked at me. Horrible.

My cheeks hurt from pretending to smile. "Wow."

"Yup. We got some calls on our tip line. We're busy chasing all of them down. I think I'll crack this case." He slapped his own knee.

I jumped.

"You're a worried Willie. Have you tried yoga?" He gestured at my mom. "You do yoga, right? I think that could really help Edan."

"She took away my phone," I growled.

Mom sighed. "I'll let you use my laptop. Only for yoga, okay? I'll know if you message your friends."

"Thanks, Mom."

"Good conversation." Garrett stood and held out his hand to my mom. "Now I have a date with a beautiful woman. No more talk about 55 gallon poly's, okay?"

29

What a strange thing to say. What was a 55 gallon poly? I barely noticed as Mom unlocked her laptop and loaded a Fightmaster Yoga video for me. I did manage to unroll Mom's pink yoga mat while I tried to process Garrett's words. I also turned up the volume to drown out any pre-date noise from my mom and Garrett in the bedroom.

"Start sitting cross-legged on your yoga mat ... " said Lesley Fightmaster on the laptop.

I did sit, breathed in and out, while opening another tab to search incognito with the computer facing me instead of our little hallway.

A 55 gallon poly was a kind of plastic barrel. It could hold 55 gallons of liquid, and poly meant plastic.

"Press your palms together and set your intention."

Now, why would Garrett Smith research the kind of plastic barrels that we'd found at Red Rock?

Sure, it could be part of his police investigation.

Or it could have started before the investigation.

When I looked up 55 gallon polys and Las Vegas, one of the top hits was a local company that sold both metal and plastic (poly) barrels. They also sold trash cans and stuff I didn't care about.[1]

What if we figured out who'd bought the barrel in Red Rock? My friends and I hadn't taken that angle, but I bet the company would remember a straightlaced Chinese lawyer type buying a barrel.

"Any intention is welcome today," said Lesley Fightmaster.

I quickly set an intention to solve Red Rock and clear my Dad's name if at all possible.

Yeah, Edward could have bought a barrel through somewhere else. I didn't have the time to chase down every single place that sold 55 gallon polys. But I could try this main company. I also marked down a few stores, or "distributors," and searched for their phone numbers so I'd be ready to call in the morning.

I quickly messaged the info to my friends using Discord, which Mom didn't know to check, where I could keep an electronic record of my research.

"Stand at the top of your mat in tadasana pose."

I finally joined in by standing in the yoga pose. It felt good to breathe and with a firm plan for tomorrow.

By the time I finished the yoga class, my friends had answered.

Callie: *Maybe Garrett's right and we should stop?*

Barstow: *Nah. Spoof your voice and your number*

The next morning, before school, Barstow helped me spoof his phone, disguising as a different number. We tested that and a voice changer by calling Callie at the pool. She hung up because she didn't recognize my voice or Barstow's number.[2]

Now all I had to do was call the barrel company.

"Ready?" said Barstow.

"Almost." I stalled long enough for Callie to join us outside the school, her hair still wet from swimming.

"I don't know," Callie said.

"All I'm doing is calling a local business," I pointed out, braver now. "I'm not chasing after anyone."

"Yeah, but what if they say they recognized your father? Will you tell Garrett?"

I shook my head. Too much of a betrayal. "One of us can call the tip line. If he's dangerous, the police need to know, but ... "

"You don't want to snitch on your own dad before you even get to say hi. I get it," said Barstow.

"Yeah," said Callie quietly, squeezing my hand once. Her fingers felt icy. I yelped, and we sort of laughed before I called the company.

It rang and rang. I crossed my fingers, half hoping they wouldn't pick up.

"Yeah?" A guy answered, right as I reached for the red button to cut the connection.

I jammed Barstow's phone back to my ear. "I need a 55 gallon drum," I told him, after an only slight delay. The voice spoofer worked. I sounded like an older man.

"Retail or wholesale?"

I glanced at my friends. Barstow held up one finger. "I only need one."

"You the same guy who came here last week? With the nose and the scars on your cheeks?"

My heart thudded in my chest. "Maybe."

He clicked his tongue. "I told ya then, I don't care if you're a foot taller than me, we don't do retail." He hung up.

My phone beeped at me, and I stared at my friends. "I only know one really tall guy who broke his nose and has acne scars."

Callie's eyes widened, and the three of us said at the same time, "Garrett Smith!"

"Could be a coincidence," Barstow admitted as we headed toward the bus circle to talk. The buses had already left, giving us a bit of privacy. "Las Vegas is a big town. There must be other tall men who've broken their noses and got acne scars."

"Yeah, but … " I thought of how Garrett never trusted anyone. How he kept telling me not to go after the Red Rock Killer.

How Garrett liked to clean up. If he shot someone, for sure he'd have a barrel ready and waiting.

"I'm scared," I said. "My mom really likes him. He comes to our place all the time. For the past two years! What if he hurts us?"

"We don't have any proof yet," said Callie. "Even if he bought a drum, it could have been for … "

Her voice trailed off. None of us could think why Garrett would need a barrel. He lives in his own one-bedroom apartment closer to the police station. Mostly he works, works out, or comes over.

"Yeesh," said Callie. "I don't know what's worse, if it's your bio dad or if it's Garrett."

"Don't say it." I felt like someone had whacked me in the stomach. I tried to breathe in and out, all yoga-like, and clear my brain out for a second.

"You could let your mom know," said Barstow.

I started to pace around them. "How? Tell her someone who looked like her boyfriend was trying to buy the murder barrel?"

"Pretty much," said Barstow. "You don't want her to be alone with him and have no idea what could happen, right? You have to warn her."

"Right." The breath poofed out of my lungs. I sucked it back in. "I better call her now."

Callie gave me her phone. We had five minutes before we had to head into school.

"Mom?" I asked as soon as she answered. "Are you okay?"

"I'm at work, Edan. Everything all right?"

"What if—" I couldn't talk. Barstow cranked his arm in a hurry up gesture, and Callie shot me an agonized look while I managed, "I'm worried. What if Garrett could be the one who hurt Mrs. Linkletter?"

"Edan Sze! What on earth—"

"Someone saw him looking for 55 gallon barrels."

"This is ridiculous, Edan. I know you don't like him, but this is a monstrous accusation."

"I know." It felt like a cold marble lodged in my throat. "I know you don't believe me, but I'm warning you in case."

"Edan, you don't need to warn me about my own boyfriend. I know him better than anyone in the world. Put this out of your mind and go to class!"

"Okay, Mom." I hung up. My fingers trembled.

Callie wrapped her arm around my shoulders and hugged me. I barely felt it.

Barstow said, "You warned her. That's the important part."

"I know." I'd said the words to my mother, but would she listen?

30

At lunch, Barstow ran at both of us with his phone. "Hey, the police scheduled another news conference!"

Was that good news? I couldn't search anything. My mother hadn't returned my phone at breakfast. *I said 24 hours and I meant 24 hours, Edan.*

While I mulled over the press conference during P.E., Foley hit me in the head with the dodgeball.[1] Technically I could stay in the game, since they don't allow head or groin hits, but I bowed out anyway.

"You okay, Edan? Are you dizzy? Sit down," urged the gym teacher.

I rubbed my forehead. I could actually feel the mark from the ball, but I felt okay. I sat on the bench, smelled people's gym clothes, and thought about the Red Rock Killer instead of my messed-up family. More relaxing.

The police kept talking to the press. That meant they had a lead, right? Or maybe they had nothing and needed help from the public.

We couldn't skip out of class for the news conference at 2 p.m., but Alicia Ramirez convinced Mr. Carver to let us listen as part of history class.

"This is what makes history, right?" Alicia used her best presentation voice.

Mr. Carver shook his head, his beard swaying from side to side. "We're supposed to cover the Great Depression."

"No one can think about the Great Depression right now. We're living it," said Alicia.

"Yeah!" Foley said.

Alicia pointed at the quote above Mr. Carver's head. "Aren't you telling us to take risks?"

We all silently read today's quote: *"Sometimes you have to risk life, in order to live, and gamble death, to sacrifice life."*— Anthony Liccione

Most of Mr. Carver's face was covered by his red beard and mustache, but his wrinkles seemed etched deeper. He opened his mouth, closed it, and made up his mind. "If you listen to the press conference, you'll have to prepare a written report about how it relates to 20th century history."

"Deal," Alicia said. "All in favor?"

Everyone but Vernon Brown stuck their hands in the air. Vernon rested his head on his desk with his eyes closed.

Alicia poked him.

Vernon blinked, registered the forest of hands up, and slowly lifted his own in the air.

"It's unanimous!" Alicia said.

Barstow, Callie, and I exchanged a quick look. Thank goodness for Alicia. Class presidents came in useful when you wanted to lie low. I aimed to stay out of the spotlight forever.

Then Mr. Carver handed me a flat box. "Before we begin, this came in the mail for you, Edan."

Huh? I hadn't ordered anything, but they'd clearly printed EDAN SZE on the address label. The package felt surprisingly light. Barstow flashed me a grin.

I remembered that he'd sent his gift to the school and beamed back. "My early birthday present! Thanks, B."

Barstow gestured at me to open it while Alicia and two other kids helped set up the laptop and projector for the press conference.

Barstow said, "Totally relevant for class, Mr. Carver. It's for the Civil War."

"For my history project," I realized aloud.

"Not 20th century history, but I approve." Mr. Carver handed me a pair of scissors.

I cut the paper tape on the sides of the shallow box and lifted out the protective cardboard covering what looked like a page cut from an old magazine.

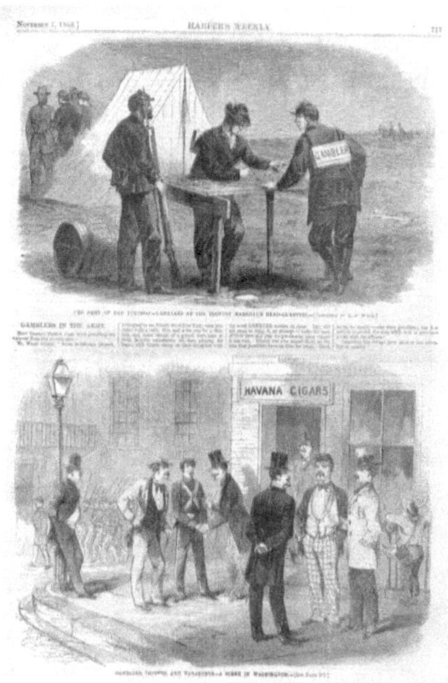

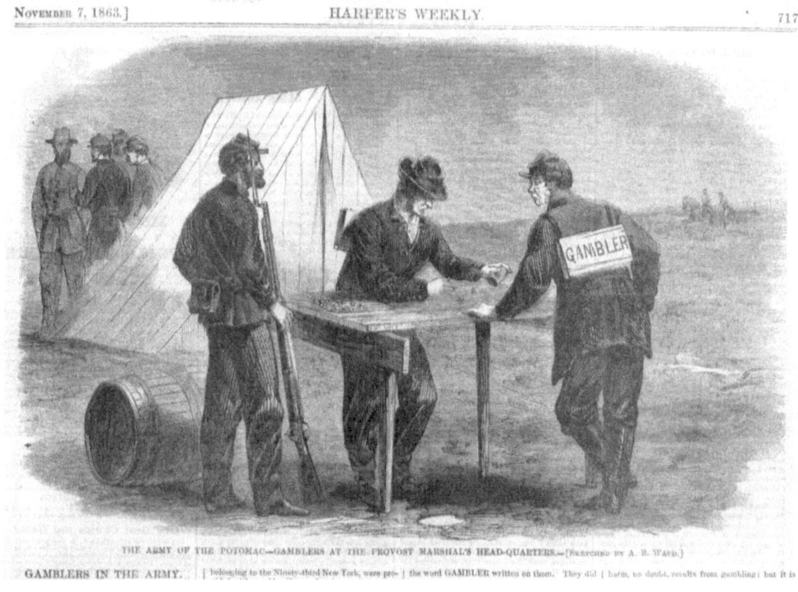

THE ARMY OF THE POTOMAC—GAMBLERS AT THE PROVOST MARSHAL'S HEAD-QUARTERS.—[SKETCHED BY A. R. WAUD.]

GAMBLERS IN THE ARMY.

The top sketch showed three men at a table. One of them clearly wore a GAMBLER sign across his back and watched as the other man seemed to empty something—dice?—out of a cup onto the table. A third man looked on, holding a very long rifle. The rifleman stood beside an empty wooden wine cask lying on its side.

Huh. I thought about the two gamblers and a guard while I glanced at the bottom sketch, which showed soldiers and men wearing top hats in front of a store that proclaimed that it carried Havana Cigars.

GAMBLERS, THIEVES, AND VAGABONDS—A SCENE IN WASHINGTON.—[See Page 711.]

I picked up the printout from the eBay seller that had come in the same package. PRINT 1863 CIVIL WAR GAMBLE ARMY THIEVES VAGABONDS. After I read the text between the two sketches, everything clicked. "Wow! The top drawing shows how General Patrick dealt with gamblers in the army. He forced them to wear GAMBLER signs while they bet on dice with beans instead of money."[2]

"Originally printed in a Harpers Weekly Magazine," said Barstow.

"Whoa. This is the real Civil War." Not only the battles, but the boring downtime when men passed the time betting on beans.

"Thanks, Barstow! Maybe we could use this as part of our Civil War reenactment, right, Mr. Carver?" I pointed at the top drawing.

Mr. Carver peered at it. He did not look thrilled under his red hair.

"Remember, you wanted to divide us into the Blue and the Grey," I told him.

"Maybe I was too hasty." Mr. Carver cracked his knuckles, the sound popping through the room.

"No, I really liked your idea of betting toothpicks on each battle. I bet Barstow would make a good general, and he and I sometimes play strategy games."

"We're starting! Get ready for the press conference." Alicia switched off the lights, dropping us into darkness.

Ava hit the projector button to share the news conference. Mr. Carver moved to the the back of the room for a better view, and the rest of us took our seats and waited for them to finish the introductions.

I carefully replaced the cardboard and the box lid over my Gamble Army Thieves Vagabonds print and slid it in my desk, mouthing my thanks at Barstow.

He smiled, and Callie gave me the thumbs up

Then I pulled out my pen and notebook just in time for the first police officer to speak.

"As you all know, the remains of Mrs. Linkletter—"

I closed my eyes, trying to block out my classmates' faces, but I could still hear their upset whispers.

"—were discovered in a barrel in the Red Rock Canyon on Saturday. The LVPD has made significant progress beyond locating and identifying Mrs. Linkletter. We have made the unfortunate discovery of another drum containing a different corpse."

We all gasped. A few of us screamed, including Alicia.

"No way!"

"What is happening?"

"Did he really say a *second* body?"

"Yes, a 'corpse.'"

"Shut the front door!"

The police continued, "We have identified this person and notified the family. Now we can share the information with the public and ask anyone withholding information to come forward. You can contact the LVPD directly or through our 24-hour hotline. The second victim has been identified as Mr. Aloysius Linkletter."

31

"Mr. Linkletter?" Alicia shouted. "But does that mean—"

"He was married to Mrs. Linkletter!" Foley answered. "He fixed our front porch."

At least three kids started crying.

"I remember him."

"He did a really good job on our basement too."[1]

"Settle down, please," said Mr. Carver, turning off the projector.

"May I go to the bathroom?" Vernon waved his hand in the air.

"I need to make sure my mom is okay!" Alicia ran for her phone in her locker. Ava and two other kids followed.

"Settle down!" Mr. Carver rushed to the land line in the corner, calling for help.

Barstow, Callie and I sat like stones.

Mr. Eisen appeared in the doorway. "What is going on?" the vice principal asked as kids streamed by him, right before Foley upended his desk. The top opened up and books and pens spilled onto the tile floor.

"They heard the news. The police found Mr. Linkletter. Deceased," Mr. Carver muttered.

"What?" Sweat glistened on Mr. Eisen's forehead. He reached for his cell phone. "This is an emergency. Calm down, everyone."

The two of them managed to corral us back in the room until 3 p.m. After the bell rang, we walked home in silence.

"Feels like a nightmare," said Callie.

"Yup," said Barstow.

"Not fun no more," I agreed. I'd heard that line on a TV show years ago, and we used it as a joke afterward. No one laughed.

Callie kicked a rock off the sidewalk and turned to face me. "You want to come to my house? In case—"

In case Garrett waited for me at my apartment. "Sure."

"I'll come too," said Barstow.

I flashed a smile at both of them. "The three musketeers." Our parents used to call us that, or EBC. Still no one laughed.

"Why would anyone want to kill Mr. Linkletter?" Callie asked.

Barstow scratched his nose. "I've been thinking about that. It could be unrelated. But since he was found in a barrel too, although in a different part of the city ... "

"It seems like the same M.O.," she agreed.

"Yup." I knew that meant modus operandi, or the same way of working. How many murderers choose to kill people named

Linkletter and stuff them into barrels? "And I don't like how they found him close to where we live."

Although they hadn't said exactly where they found him, they did say it was in the Meadows area, which is our neck of the woods and pretty close to the Springs Preserve.

Callie wrapped her ponytail around her fingers. "Like the person's getting closer and closer!"

"Unless it's a copycat killer," Barstow pointed out.

"Ugh! Why did you say that?" Callie pretended to shove him.

"There are whack jobs who see how famous killers get and try to imitate them," he insisted.

Callie shuddered. So did I.

"It could be someone who wants to be famous, or infamous," I agreed. Another vocabulary word for me. "And maybe some tourist wants to hurt people here. But two Linkletters? That's got to be someone who knows them, right? Which means it's probably someone WE know."

A car grumbled past with a loud engine. Barstow moved closer to the inside of the sidewalk and said, "It's usually someone close to the family. Have we checked out the three Linkletter kids at all?"

"No!" Callie rubbed her eyes.

"Well, we probably should." Barstow didn't apologize.

"That makes sense," I said quietly, "but I think Callie is too upset."

"We should all be upset," she said.

"I am too, but I want to clear my dad if I can."

They nodded at that.

I said, in a smaller voice, "I need to figure out if Garrett did it."

None of us spoke. A car passed us playing hymns, and someone else honked a horn.

Barstow said, "Edan, you're not doing this alone. Callie, you can chill, but I'll research the Linkletter kids. Edan, you want to take your dad and Garrett?"

I bit my lip. Barstow was always logical. I didn't want to complain, but ... "That leaves me alone with Edward and Garrett."

"It won't take me long with the Linkletter kids," said Barstow. "If they're innocent, I can rule them out. The police must have already looked at their alibis. Then I can help you. Sound good?"

"I don't know."

Callie sighed. "I want to help you, but I don't know either."

I reached for my phone that wasn't there. I breathed in and out, steadying myself, before I turned to Barstow. "I've been putting off reaching out to my father. You gave me his address. I'd better start there."

"I'm coming with you," Callie said, even though we'd landed in front of her neat, white bungalow, and the Linkletters' deaths had creeped her out.

I shook my head. "You go home. You wanted to get away from this."

Callie tugged at her ponytail. "I won't be able to take a nap if you're meeting your dad alone!"

"Me neither," said Barstow. "It's all of us or nothing. I'll check out the Linkletters' kids later."

I breathed a sigh of relief at both of them. "Thanks."

"So you have his address on you?" Barstow asked.

I nodded. I'd copied every scrap of Edward Wong info onto my phone, plus kept the written version tucked in my pocket where my emergency $20 used to live.

I'd even mapped out my dad's office, secretly planning to go there. Now I showed them the recommended route I'd scrawled down. "Sorry, it takes 1.5 hours to bus it over."[2]

Callie made a face but patted my shoulder. "He lives in Green Valley, so I'm not surprised his office is past Sunset Park."

Barstow whipped out his phone and scrolled through the directions. "It's not that bad. We'll head south on the 104 and then switch to the 212 to go east on East Sunset. Pretty easy."

Callie ran ahead of us to hold the 104, a lucky break because bus times don't match the app half the time. We chugged after her, climbed on, and beeped our passes.

After we finished catching our breath, Barstow checked the time. "He should be there now. You want to call first?"

"I guess. To make sure he's in." I glanced at the other people on the bus, even though no one should care. One woman chatted on her Bluetooth. Another nodded off over her groceries. Five guys of varying ages either listened to music or glued their eyes to their own phones.

"I can call for you," said Callie, but I knew I had to do it.

"Just give me a minute." I inhaled, exhaled, thought of the Linkletters, and tapped the digits before I stopped again.

Callie lifted her finger, raising her eyebrows like a question. I let her press the call button for me.

It rang three times before a man's voice said, "Hello, you have reached the office of Edward Wong, LLB, complex litigator and certified fraud examiner. Please leave a message and we will return your call as soon as possible. You may also email us at info at Justicelitigation.com. Thank you."

I hung up and stared at my phone. Was that my father's voice? Had I waited over 13 years to hear this?

I hung up without leaving a message. I couldn't speak.

32

We didn't talk much as we switched buses and walked the last bit down North Green Valley Parkway and past their very nice library and civic centre.

"Could've ride shared," muttered Barstow.

"But we couldn't risk it," Callie said. "You want another ride record making its way back to your parents? I don't."

Barstow didn't say another word, except to glance inside a diner that recommended we come in to "feed your inner bear."

"Hits different when we've got a killer on the loose," I said, and we all laughed a little. Finally.

The last time we'd gone on a trek like this, we'd found the barrel at Red Rock. None of us wanted to admit that.

We reached my father's building, a skyscraper with silvery-blue windows. The sun burnt my eyes as its rays bounced off the reflective glass.

Cars and trucks parked neatly in their white-lined spaces in front of the building. Strange to think that one of them might belong to my dad. Even stranger to think I might meet my dad himself in the next few minutes.

"You okay?" asked Callie.

"I'm alive."

She side-hugged me so tight that I could feel her breathing. Barstow stood by within arm's reach, close enough to touch, which was like a hug from him. When I finally stepped away, I said, "Thanks. Seriously. I couldn't do this without you."

"Sure you could," said Barstow. "It would just suck."

Callie's laugh floated through the air.

"Suck more," I agreed. And we all laughed this time, mostly to delay going in.

"You know he may not be there," said Barstow.

"Or in a meeting," Callie said.

"I know. I don't care. I've got to try." My palms hurt, and I made myself unclench my fists. My nails left grooves in my palms.

We all filed into one section of the rotating door, even though it mashed us together, especially with our back packs. Still, it felt better squished together than apart.

A huge guard stuffed into a suit silently watched us come in.

I marched right up to the mute guard. *No fear.* "Hello, I'm here to see the lawyer, Edward Wong."

The man's expression stayed blank. That seemed like a rich

building thing, to hire robotic employees. "Whom shall I say is calling?" he asked.

Wow. Whom. I almost said "His daughter." But Edward's other kids were sons, which the guard might know (another rich building thing!), so I replied, "Amy Sze's daughter and friends."

The guard dialled and spoke in a low voice on the phone, turning his shoulder away from us.

Callie and I held hands until the guard nodded and said, "Eighth floor, turn left, and he's in suite 8050."

We walked into the elevator, acting cool, but with me sweating. As soon as the elevator doors closed, I asked, "Do I stink? Do I have anything stuck between my teeth?" I bared my teeth at them.

"No stinking," Callie assured me.

"Your teeth look okay," said Barstow.

"Cute outfit too," said Callie.

I made a face. "I wouldn't have worn my yellow spelling bee T-shirt[1] if I'd known I might meet my dad." I'd grabbed one of my only clean shirts.

Barstow shrugged. "It'll give you something to talk about. If my dad just met me, he'd be stoked to find out I was a spelling bee champion."

"You *are* a spelling bee champion," I said. Barstow beat me the year after.

"And my father is stoked about it."

The elevator door dinged open. For a second, I froze. Callie and Barstow each grabbed an arm and towed me out as my feet dragged behind us.

"I'm not ready for this," I whispered to them.

"You were born ready," said Callie, and I had to laugh. She psyched herself up for swim meets by chanting stuff like that, and I guess it worked, because my feet started moving again.

The whole building oozed money: the guard, the spotless stainless steel elevator doors, the cameras in the hallways, the classy lighting, the art on the hallway walls. I stared at one print of splotches of red and white and black. Kind of nice. Did my dad pick it out?[2]

"Just act normal," Barstow told me.

"I am."

"Since when did you look at art?"

"I look at the split screens on video games. That's art."

"Noted," said Callie, pointing at the grey door marked 8050.

I squeezed my eyes shut. *I can do this.*

Can I do this?

My friends would knock even if I didn't.

And my dad was waiting for me.

I knocked.

33

"Come. In," drawled a man's voice through the wood. My father? Did my dad talk a bit like the sloth in Zootopia?[1] Barstow tossed open the door.

I stared at a Black male wearing enormous glasses. "Hel-lo," he said slowly and precisely.

Not my dad. At least not unless I'd lost some melanin along the way. "Hi, my name is Edan Sze. I'm here to see Edward Wong."

"Do you have an appointment?"

I could practically swim in the spaces between his words, but he was wearing the most expensive suit I'd ever seen, so he must know what he was doing. "My mother is Amy Sze. We called up and he agreed to see me."

Mr. Sloth gestured at my friends, unspeaking.

"These are my best friends, Callie Yang and Barstow Ness. They're here to protect me. I mean ... " *Ugh.*

"You don't need protecting from Mr. Wong," said Mr. Sloth.

Maybe I do! I thought, but didn't say.

"We've followed Edan's journey from the beginning," said Barstow, who'd lowered his voice to sound older.

I raised my eyebrows at Barstow's weird voice. Was that supposed to convince this man to let in my very mature friends?

Mr. Sloth migrated toward the door. Maybe to kick us out?

"Excuse me—" I started.

Callie refused to move out of Mr. Sloth's way. Instead, she offered her most magnetic smile. "This is a once in a lifetime opportunity for Mr. Wong to meet Miss Edan Sze."[2]

That was so strange that it made Mr. Sloth literally stop in his tracks. "Once. In a. Lifetime?"

"Absolutely," said Callie. "We've come all this way to discuss a complex case. This opportunity won't come again."

Barstow and I held our breath. It sounded bizarre to me, but she's got the magic touch with adults. Better let her work her spell.

Mr. Sloth looked us up and down. I truly wished I'd worn a suit instead of my yellow spelling bee T-shirt, black pants, sports socks, and running shoes with holes at each big toe.

At long last, Mr. Sloth eked out, "Let me. See. What Mr. Wong. Has to. Say." He dawdled back to his desk to pick up his phone.

The three of us didn't look at each other while Mr. Sloth

murmured into the receiver, but after what felt like two hours, he gestured for us to follow him. "Just you," he said, pointing at me.

I hesitated, glancing at my friends to gauge their reactions. Should I insist? Or would that force Mr. Sloth to kick all of us out?

"Those are his conditions," said Mr. Sloth. "He will only see Amy Sze's daughter, for 15 minutes maximum."

"Are you sure?" I stalled, but Mr. Sloth wouldn't back down.

So this was it. Splitting EBC up again, right before meeting Edward Wong.

"Okay." I nodded at Mr. Sloth, but before I fell into step behind him, I met my friends' eyes and silently asked them to watch out for me. To have my back. To come get me if I didn't show my face within 15 minutes.

Their eyes told me, without words, that I didn't have to ask.

I followed Mr. Sloth down an inner corridor lined with what looked like grey material. I touched it as I passed, leaving my DNA, silently wondering if I should etch my name into it in case I never got out of here alive.

In case I walked toward the Red Rock Killer.

34

Mr. Sloth tapped the door at the end of the corridor before easing it open. I couldn't resist poking my head in the gap, even if it meant my own death.

"Dad?" My mouth formed the word silently as I stared at the man inside, who had his back to us so he could stare out the glass window.

I clocked his dark hair cut short at the nape of the neck, like you'd expect in a lawyer, especially one who demanded matching socks.

Nice neck, tanned and not too flabby. Seriously expensive-looking suit.

Was this my father?

Mr. Sloth intoned, "Mr. Wong. May I—"

My father turned, and the shock of recognition banged me in the chest. *I looked like him.*[1]

"—present—"

I had my dad's eyes. Not his nose, or slightly pointed chin, but our dark eyes—

"—Miss—"

—and even our cheekbones matched in a way that my mother's and mine never had.

"Edan Sze."

Mr. Wong's eyes widened, so I knew he'd caught the resemblance too.

Should I run at him, hug his legs, and say, "Daddy Daddy Daddy"? No, I was too old.[2]

So I dug my nails back into my palms and thought about how handsome he was, with a just-right nose, enough to give him character without anyone calling him a knuckle nose. Lips that looked like they smiled a lot. No beard or mustache.

I glanced at his hands. Nope, no match with those strong, thick fingers or with that height. I seemed more Mom-sized.

But overall, even without a DNA test, I knew I stood in the presence of my biological father.

"Hello," he said.

I laughed. I couldn't help it. After almost 14 years of missing each other, him unaware that I existed, and me not knowing a shred of detail about him, what else could we say?

"Hi," I managed, and we chuckled together while the door clicked closed behind Mr. Sloth.

"Edan, is it?" My father pronounced my name exactly right, Eeed'n. "It's ... good to see you. I didn't know about you."

"Yeah. My mom kept me a secret until now."

He tilted his head to the right, processing that, and I got another zing. Callie once took a picture of me thinking, looking exactly like that.

My father didn't ask me why Mom hadn't told him, or why she'd changed her mind now. I could practically feel his brain synapses blasting, but he kept calm.

"I'm glad you're here now," he said. "I would have liked to watch you grow up."

I blinked back tears. I didn't expect to like him, this lawyer who'd abandoned me and my mom. The man who could have killed Mrs. L, no matter how unlikely that felt.

"What should I call you?" I asked.

He shook his head, not like he was impatient, but like I'd asked the wrong question. "What's your opinion on that?"

"Well, it would be weird to call you Dad or Father right off the bat. Do you like Mr. Wong, Edward, Eddie, or complex litigator?"

He smiled. "It's good that you have a sense of humour. You can call me any of the above. I want you to feel comfortable with me."

"Well, you probably don't want me to call you Dad. You have a new family now."

His eyebrows gathered together. "I'll have to talk to them first. It will be a big shock. Still, call me what you want."

"Oh." I pressed my hand to my throat. I didn't want to cry. He seemed so nice! Could he really have hurt anyone?

He did hurt my mother.

"Would you like to meet my wife and my sons?" he asked.

"I—I don't know." I gulped.

He smiled. "It doesn't have to be a sit-down meal. We could go to a show, or eat, or listen to music. What kind of things do you like?"

"Um. Stardew Valley."

A smile flashed across his face. "Yes, my boys like it too. And Minecraft and Roblox."

Happiness glinted inside me. I didn't have to explain that Stardew was a video game! "Terraria."

He rolled his eyes. "A little violent for them, but I've played it."

"You have?" My mom refuses.

"With my friends. But if I play PvE—"

Player vs. Environment. A whole piece of myself unfolded in front of my eyes. Was my dad what I'd missed my whole life?

"—I usually like World of Warcraft and games like that, which are too old for you."[3] He frowned slightly. "I hope. How old are you?"

"I turn 14 on August 30th."

He counted back in his head. "That works. Yes." He paused to think, which reminded me of Mr. Sloth. Then Dad asked a more important question. "How is your mother?"

"She's fine. She runs and—" I tried to think of what else, besides Garrett. *Writes in her diary. Takes away my phone.* "—works for the police."

"Works for the police!"

"As a secretary. You don't have to join the LVPD to do administrative work. She jokes that she'd never pass the physical."

He shook his head in amazement. "I never thought she'd give up on her dreams."

"Well, you know." I pointed at myself. "Kind of hard to act with a kid."

Awkwardness zapped him for the first time. He'd taken everything in stride so far, maybe because he was used to surprises in his work. Now he tried to patch it up. "That's true. Do you like to act too?"

I shrugged. "I like dancing better."

"Ah, you take dance lessons? What kind?" His spark returned. "I don't know much about that. My boys won't."

I shook my head. "Dance lessons cost money."

He winced.

"Also, you can learn a lot for free on YouTube."

He stood up and leaned against his desk, accidentally bopping the mouse cable, but neither of us cared. "I bet. You'll have to teach me."

"You don't want a paternity test first?"

He rubbed his forehead with his thumb. "Yes, well, there's a whole protocol to follow in paternity suits, which we should do."

My heart plunged like it had jumped out the window without me. I knew it was too good to be true. I stared at the holes in my sneakers.

"But for now, Edan, if you want me to dance on YouTube—"

I smiled. I couldn't help it. He was so much nicer and cooler than I'd expected. "I don't livestream or anything. I'm not that good."

"Thank goodness."

"I do TikToks though. The easy dances."

Dad laughed. "I've done a few Tiktoks, but gaming ones."

"I do gaming ones too. That's my most popular one! No one cares if I dance, but I do it because I like it."[4]

His eyes glowed. "We have a lot in common. Do you like hiking?"

Hiking. I shot back to that Saturday with the lemony smell of the trees, brushing sand out of my shoes, and the barrel.

"No!" I hollered.

Dad stared at me, horrified. Up until that second, we'd clicked, but hiking meant Red Rock. And Mrs. Linkletter. And Mr. Linkletter.

My heart battered my chest. I couldn't speak. Couldn't explain. Mr. Sloth knocked on the door. "Mr. Wong?"

"Excuse me." Dad opened the door to talk to Mr. Sloth, but Callie stuck her head in the gap under his arm.[1] "Are you okay, Edan? Say something!"

"Yes, I'm okay! Just surprised." I joined my father at the door. Mr. Sloth frowned, but I asked, "Do you mind if my friends Callie and Barstow come in?"

"I don't mind, but what are you all doing here?" Dad asked.

"My apologies, sir," said Mr. Sloth. "The children ran down the hall when they heard their friend shout."

"Are you okay?" Barstow called from behind Mr. Sloth.

"Yeah, he said something that surprised me, but no one's hurting me."

Barstow eyed me up and down before he backed away, giving Callie the time to size me up. She raised her eyebrows as a question, and I half smiled with a thumbs up.

"You said these are your friends, Edan," said Dad.

I shivered. I really liked hearing him say my name. But what if he was the bad guy? "Yeah, these are my best friends in the whole world, Carrie[2] and Ben." I deliberately fudged their names, which made them pause, but they nodded.

Dad opened the door and shook both their hands, surprising all of us. "Then they're my friends too. Would you like them to come in, or do you want time with your friends, Edan?"

"Both." I had to wipe my eyes.

Barstow and Callie hurried inside. "You okay?" Callie asked again, while Barstow muttered, "Aight?" like his dad.

"How can I help?" my own father asked.

I took a deep breath. "I need to ask you a question with just you, me, and my friends." I jerked my chin at Mr. Sloth. "If you don't mind waiting outside, please."

Dad didn't know how to react, but after minute, he said, "Of course. Gerald, if you don't mind waiting in the corridor?"

I had to smile a tiny bit. Gerald. Good name for Mr. Sloth.

I waited for the door to swing shut behind him. Then I glanced at my friends to gather up my courage, fisted my hands, and whispered, "Were you the last person who saw Mrs. Linkletter alive?"

36

My friends sucked in their breaths.

We all watched my father's reaction.

Dad glanced out the window, but not like he was trying to escape. More like he was thinking.

Finally, he said, "I'm not able to disclose information sometimes. I don't know if you know this, but I work under very strict rules."

Barstow held up a finger. "Attorney-client privilege."

Dad gave a sharp nod. "That's right. I'm not saying that anyone was my client or not, only that I can't tell you everything because my job's rules mean that I'm sworn to secrecy. Even more than a doctor or a priest."

"Really?" Callie asked.

"Really. If you brought a priest or doctor to court, you could force them to answer questions under cross-examination. I could refuse to answer the same questions because I can't break an oath to my client."[1]

"So you can't tell us anything?" Barstow asked.

Dad tilted his head from side to side. "I wouldn't say that. We can talk about Terraria."

Barstow cracked a smile.

Callie didn't. "Then you could have hurt Mrs. Linkletter, and you could claim attorney-client privilege afterward."

Dad thought about this. "I can see that you don't trust me. I understand that. Trust is something I have to earn. The problem is, I can't earn it by breaking the rules of my profession."

I could see that he took his work seriously, which I liked. On the other hand, did he use the law as a shield, like Callie said?

"You're a complex litigator, right?" I asked.

Dad nodded. "Exactly right."

The three of us looked at each other before I asked the next obvious question. "What does that mean?"

"I work with clients here, across the U.S., and around the world. I have expertise in banking, real estate, entertainment, construction—"

Construction. Maybe he met Mr. Linkletter?

"—and pharmaceutical industries. I can supervise and coordinate experts in large litigation cases or damage claims."

What? I didn't really understand that. My friends' eyes glazed over too, but none of us interrupted.

"I'm certified both in Nevada and in Hong Kong, where I spent most of my time until recently. I'm a Certified Fraud Examiner with a special interest in corporate fraud and business law."

That seemed like another dead end. I was pretty sure Mrs. Linkletter had never been to Hong Kong. She told us all about her trip to New Jersey on the morning announcements, so HK should have ranked much higher.

"Would you tell us if Mrs. Linkletter *wasn't* your client?" asked Callie.

"I find it best not to name anyone. Finances and litigation are a very personal matter."

Barstow, who'd started scrolling through his phone, shook his head. "I'm pretty sure that's not what the legal society makes you do here."

"I always follow the legal society's regulations, but it's up to every individual attorney to make up his, her, or their own personal code of conduct. I find it's better to exceed confidentiality. That way you run into fewer problems."

Darn. He made sense.

Dad watched us, his eyes lingering on me. "I assume your curiosity relates to your strong reaction to my question about hiking?"

Wait, did he slip in that hiking question on purpose? Did he know that we were the ones who had found that barrel in Red Rock?

We all watched Dad, stunned, like he'd confessed to killing Mrs. L. Callie squeezed my hand, and after a second, I realized Barstow had grabbed her arm too.

We faced him together. *Don't kill us. Don't kill us.*

Dad raised his eyebrows and coughed out a laugh. "I've already told you that I like following rules and set my own guidelines that are even stricter. Do you really think I would break the most serious rule and take someone's life?"

"Mmph," said Barstow.

"You seem awfully convincing," Callie muttered. She's used to running rings around most grown-ups.

I lifted my chin and told him, "I don't know."

Dad's lips parted. I could tell that my opinion was important to him, whether he'd admit it or not.

"Some people obey the rules and then break them," I pointed out. "One guy in our class was really polite, but when we heard about Mr. Linkletter, he overturned his desk. No warning."

Dad's lips quivered. Was he squeezing down a laugh? I scowled at him. I wasn't aiming for funny.

"I'm sorry. Thanks for sharing that with me."

I bet he got practice saying that with his two sons. Which wasn't a bad thing.

"I don't like to disobey rules in general, even when under great stress, Edan," said Dad. "I recognize that I don't have any good way to prove that to you and that all you have right now is my word. I want you to understand what kind of person I am without answering questions that would end my career. What can I do?"

Barstow met his eyes. "Can you tell us where you were from 3 p.m on Thursday to 8 a.m. on Saturday?"

Dad thought about this for way too long. Finally, he spoke. "You'd have to ask my family."

Dad said other stuff, like inviting us to a BBQ at his house tomorrow, but it kind of blurred in my brain. As we descended in the smooth, silent elevator, I realized that we left my dad almost no wiser than we had been before. Except for one thing.

When we hit the sidewalk outside his office, Callie said, "I don't think he did it." She touched a band's poster on the telephone pole.

Yep. That was the thing. I smiled at her, and she grinned back at me.

"What makes you say that?" Barstow asked, jabbing the pedestrian cross button with his elbow.

Callie tossed her hair. "He's a lawyer who can't talk because of attorney-client privilege, but he's a good guy. I don't think he killed anyone."

I nodded. That was my feeling too. Unscientific but true.[2]

"So where was he the night that Mrs. L disappeared?" Barstow asked.

I sighed. "I guess I could ask his family, like he said?" I could hear the hollowness in my own voice.

"Well, he invited us to a BBQ with them right after that," Callie said. "It's not like he's hiding them from you. He said me and Barstow could come! And your mom and Garrett."

"That's true." Dad had even smiled when I'd said Mom had a boyfriend.

Then I shook my head. I could maybe picture my mom making peace with my dad, but Garrett? Mr. 55 Gallons himself? "Actually, I haven't figured out why Garrett wants a barrel. So he's not off the hook. And he definitely doesn't get to meet my dad."

"So complicated," Callie groaned.

I nodded. At least the light changed, so we got to move. A lime green sports car revved its engine at us. We ignored it.

"What do you think, Edan?" Callie asked. "It's your dad."

"That's what makes it even harder. I want to be objective like Barstow and figure out if he had means, motive, and opportunity, but I keep getting hung up on the fact that he's my father and he kind of smells the same as me. You know what I mean?"

"Yeah, I thought something reeked in there," said Barstow, and I punched his shoulder.

"I'm serious."

He laughed. "Just trying to lighten it up in here."

"By telling me we smell?"

"Exactly."

We chuckled. Even bad jokes make you feel better when you're in deep doo doo.

Barstow didn't trust my dad. Callie did, but she trusts most people. I sighed. Liking him wasn't quite the same as trusting him.

But I could gather evidence and get to know him better, especially at this BBQ with his family.

"That's it!" I punched the air. A guy waiting for the bus shuffled away from us.

"My dad gave me a hint!"

"What are you talking about?" Callie squinted into the late day sun.

"He's bound by attorney-client privilege, but his family isn't. They're not lawyers. Or even if they are, they don't work there." I jerked my thumb back at his tower. "The Linkletters aren't his wife and kids' clients. He invited us to that BBQ at his house tomorrow so that they can clear his name!"

37

The only snag in my little plan? Telling my mom once I got home.

"You're going to a BBQ with your father and his family?" Mom looked completely bamboozled when I sprang it on her after supper, near the kitchen sink. "How is that possible? You don't even know him."

"I'm sorry. Um, you and G—I mean, you're invited too, if that makes you feel any better."

"It does not! I haven't spoken to Eddie in over fourteen years. You don't know him either. He could be an—" She censored herself, biting down on her bottom lip. "A terrible person!"

"He's not."

"How would you know?"

"I talked to him. That's why he invited me. Us."

Steam practically burst out of both of her ears. "What?"[1]

"It was a spur of the moment thing when we got out early from school. I took the bus to his office in Green Valley. Totally safe."

"You already met him! Without me? By yourself?" She gripped the kitchen counter so hard that her knuckles really did turn white.

Ooh boy. How could I make her feel better? "No, with Barstow and Callie. EBC. The three musketeers, you know?"

"You three children took the bus on your own? When there's a killer around?"

And it could be my own father, my brain added automatically, although I don't think so. I'd have to prove it by collecting a real alibi for him.

"That is not okay, Edan. You're supposed to ask me before you go anywhere besides school or home."

"Mom, I'm almost fourteen ... "

"I don't care how old you are. Vegas is not safe, especially right now. You don't have good judgement. Your frontal lobe isn't completely developed!"

Sometimes she's pretty random. "Okay. Sorry. I'm okay, though. Can I go to the BBQ?"[2]

She shook her head. "What did I tell you? *No further investigation.*"

"Mom! I don't have to talk to him about the deceased." Although I would talk to his family. Maybe that showed in my face.

"I'm very angry at you right now, Edan. I can't trust you or Callie or Barstow. You are fully and completely grounded. No phone. No screens at all for 48 hours."

"Mom, you're going to keep me away from my own father?" I choked on what I wanted to say next: *You've already kept him away from me for almost a decade and a half.* "He wants to see me. He wants to get to know me. And now I can't even tell him I'm not going to the BBQ?"

"I'll tell him," she snapped back.

"You—"

She pointed her finger at me and held the other hand out for my phone. I left it on the kitchen table instead of handing it over directly. My one piece of defiance.

Then I beat it back to—well, I didn't HAVE a room, so I slammed the bathroom door, locking myself in a tiny cell of space with a toilet, a shower stall, and a sink so close together that I could touch them all at once if I sat on the throne and stuck out my left leg and my right hand.

I stood there, refusing to meet my own eyes in the chipped mirror, where the lighting cast weird shadows all over my face. The face that looked so much like my father's and would remind me what I missed.

My life was over. I couldn't even tell my friends why I'd cut them off. My dad would think I'd abandoned him too, unless Mom filled him in.

Grounded. Jailed like Rapunzel in her tower. Tomorrow was Saturday—no school—so for 48 hours, I wouldn't leave these four walls.

Shoot, that reminded me. I'd forgotten Barstow's present in my desk. During the next two days of boredom, I could've studied that CIVIL WAR GAMBLE ARMY THIEVES VAGABONDS print and fit it into my presentation.

Instead, imprisonment.

What if the apartment caught on fire? I dug in my pocket to text that to Mom, only to have my phoneless state hit me again. Ugh!

In a fire, would I have to knot bedsheets together and climb down from the second floor window of our living room or her bedroom? This bathroom didn't even *have* a window.

Don't be so dramatic, Mom's voice sounded in my head.

I exhaled. In a fire, I could still call 911, or anyone else, with our kitchen landline. Weird. Very old school, but still possible.

And I should probably take the stairs in a fire, the way we'd practiced since I was a little kid.

I'd have to leave the bathroom to do that, though.

38

Garrett showed up that night as I unfolded the couch to make my bed. Mom had insisted on taking over the bathroom to prep for him, leaving us alone together.

I held my breath and set the metal frame on the ground. I pressed the mattress flat, avoiding his eyes.

Finally, Garrett spoke. "I heard you got yourself into a bit of trouble today."

I looked him straight in the eye as I shook out my blankets, even though my insides quaked. "I met my dad."

"Without your mother's knowledge or permission. Do you understand why that's wrong?"

I did understand, even if I thought it was very unfair. I'd brought my friends, and we were in public most of the time.

"Amy wanted to give you time to adjust to the idea of your father. You've always been close. She thought you'd come to her as soon as you were ready. Instead, you headed off without telling her. You put all three of you at risk by walking around the city when we haven't yet put the Red Rock Killer behind bars."

I stared at my toes. I would never want to risk my friends' lives. I love them more than anything.

"You think you're a police officer in training, but police work is teamwork.[1] We rely on each other. Even if we're not driving together, another officer is only one radio call away. We're trained not only to use our weapons and prepare for combat, but also how to de-escalate a situation.[2] That means we know how to talk to people, how to negotiate, and when to let something go."

I felt like crying now. All I wanted to do was help and to meet my dad. I'd done it. No one got hurt.

But I knew what he was saying. It could have gone sideways, especially since my dad was still a potential suspect. I rubbed my nose, wiling myself not to cry.

Garrett dropped his voice. "I'm not trying to make you feel bad, Edan. I want you to understand how dangerous this was, and to promise me you'll never do this again."

Would Sherlock Holmes make that promise? But he was a fictional character from another century, and Garrett had a point. I had no idea what I was doing. I'd been winging it the whole time.

I nodded and patted my pillows in place, avoiding his eyes.

"I need you to say it out loud, Edan."

"Okay." I sniffed hard and rubbed my eyes with the back of my hand before grabbing a tissue from the box on our dining room table.

"I care about you and your mother. I want to watch you grow up. I want you to be safe, that's all." He sounded gruff now too.

"Okay," I whispered, and he finally left.

39

"You're 100 percent grounded for 48 hours? No way," said Callie at 9 a.m. on Saturday morning. Garrett and Mom hadn't reappeared from her bedroom, and I couldn't sleep, so I'd quietly called her on the landline in the kitchen, knowing Callie was an early bird.

"Way," I said glumly. We'd learned that slang from an old Saturday Night Live sketch.[1]

It felt hollow, talking audio-only to one friend instead of two. Callie never got grounded, since she loved following the rules. Barstow generally avoided trouble, but not because he was a people pleaser. More because he was too smart to get caught.

"I can help. Want me to tell your dad you'll miss the BBQ?" Callie asked. "You still have his number on a piece of paper, right? I could leave a message at his office too."

"No, Mom said she'd do it. And I only have his home number written down, not his office." I could do it myself, but Mom might flip about any "further investigation."

"Well, I can catch you up on something else. I heard Mr. Eisen won't come to school on Monday. He's going on stress leave."

"Whoa. Mr. Eisen?" Our vice principal did seem kind of jittery, now that she mentioned it.

"Yeah, Mr. Linkletter tipped him over the edge. Also something about how the school's budget is all messed up."

"Huh?"

"Yeah. Someone embezzled a bunch of money."

"From our school?" Forester Middle School isn't fancy, and we don't live in a rich part of Las Vegas. If thieves were going to sneak in, they should pick a school in Summerlin or Henderson or, well, Green Valley.[2]

"I know it sounds crazy, but my mom said something about forensic accountants."

"And Mr. Eisen has something to do with it?"

"Maybe? Barstow might know. His mom told my mom."

"Okay, I'll call him after."

"My parents are losing it. No principal, no VP, and now no money."

Shoot. Of course Mrs. Linkletter had done a lot more than say "Good morning, Foresters," and ask after Ava's goldfish. Her work had been kind of invisible to me before. "Oh, man."

"School will still open on Monday, though. That's what Barstow says."

"I better call him. Thanks." I hung up the phone and switched to my other ear. My arm had cramped up while talking to Callie. How did people talk for hours on these things in the olden days? Luckily, Barstow picked up almost right away, and I said, "Hey."

"Hey." His voice sounded muffled.

I pressed the receiver against my ear, trying to hear better. You can't turn up the volume on a landline. "You okay?"

"Yeah. I wanted to check something out."

"What? Listen, my mom and Garrett completely lost it on me—"

"Yeah, Callie texted me. There's something else going on, though."

"What's that?" I gripped the receiver tighter.

"We have to figure out why someone would want to kill Mr. and Mrs. Linkletter."

"Yeah, totally."

"Your dad didn't have a good motive. Why would he attack a client?"

My heart thumped. I hated hearing my friend say it, even in theory.

"Your dad clearly had opportunity," said Barstow. "Chances are, he was the last person to see her alive. Lots of people in Vegas carry guns, so he'd have means."

"What are you saying?" I hissed into the phone. "You think it's my dad, or don't you?"

"I need to check out a few more things before I say anything. Don't worry about it. You're grounded. Sit tight and don't get killed."

"Not funny. You be careful too, Barstow. Callie said someone stole money from the school."

He chuckled, almost like a snort. "Someone did steal money. Remember how we both lost twenty bucks? Me from my desk and you from your front pocket?"

Sure did. I hadn't asked my mother to replace mine yet, especially not while I was grounded twice. "Yeah."

"I baited our desks."

"What?"

"Someone stole money from my desk, so I left another $20 with a trap using a security camera and theft detection powder. Yours only has the powder. It'll literally catch the thief red-handed. Or purple-handed, the powder said."

"What? You made a trap? Is that even legal?"

He snorted. "I gotta go see if it went off. Then we'll have our answers."

"No, Barstow! Call the police. That's their job. Or let me or Callie call them!"

But calling the cops was the one thing Barstow would never do. He hung up on me.

40

"Callie!" I punched in every digit of her number because it wasn't saved in our landline phone.[1]

Luckily, she picked up right away. "Edan?"

"Barstow's flying off to school to catch the thief. You need to stay on him, or get his parents—"

"I'll stay on him."

"But Garrett said—"

Callie cut the call. She probably needed to call Barstow, but it still made me ragey. I slammed my own phone down, just so I'd have something to do and because the old, plastic phones can handle abuse.

That felt good except Mom and Garrett would freak.

I ducked my head and listened to our tap drip.

Hmm. I tightened the kitchen faucet, ears on alert. Normally my mother's bat hearing would kick in. I tiptoed toward her closed door and reached for a note stuck to the door.

> *Edan,*
>
> *Garrett and I are going out for brunch. Use the landline to call us in an emergency. You're still grounded. Don't leave the apartment or use screens for any reason. I changed the Wifi password anyway.*
>
> *Don't invite Callie or Barstow over.*
>
> *I left a message for your father that you're not coming to his house today.*
>
> *I love you. Have some cereal for breakfast. I'll bring you a blueberry muffin.[2]*
>
> *Love,*
>
> *Mom*

Garrett had scrawled his name under hers. He'd obviously read the note too, which seemed like none of his business.

Okay, never mind that. I had to help Barstow.

What was he thinking?

How could he break into school on a Saturday? Then I remembered that they have track and field on the weekend. Plus Barstow might disarm the alarm and sneak inside even if it was locked. He was that smart.

So now I needed to get into his head.

Who'd want to kill Mr. and Mrs. Linkletter?

Hang on. It was actually *Mrs.* Linkletter first, then Mr. Linkletter.

Did that make a difference? Mr. Eisen had left too, which seemed sort of suspicious.

I backed up to the thief at school. Did Barstow figure the same person stole money from his desk?

My cash could've fallen out of my pocket. Or did someone *pickpocket* me?

I wrinkled my nose. I hadn't hugged any of my classmates, and didn't get near anyone except Barstow and Callie.

But I'd taken my pants off in gym class and forgotten to move the money to my shoe, which had a hole in it anyway. Anyone could have stolen it.

I gave up on the thief angle and moved onto opportunity. Who had seen Mrs. L last?

Everyone at the PTA meeting. Me. Mr. L.

Then, if Mr. L had been telling the truth (and why would he lie?), my father.

My father was a lawyer. Was it possible either he'd met Mrs. L about something lawyer-y, even at night?

The only reason to go after hours was for privacy. Either for her privacy or for his. Let's say Mrs. L insisted she meet my dad after hours because she didn't want anyone else to know.

I didn't understand my dad's job enough to figure out why someone would have killed Mrs. Linkletter post meeting, but I realized something else.

If my dad wasn't guilty, then he was in danger.

Because he was the only person who knew the Linkletters' secret. And he was the only one legally sworn never to tell anyone.

41

The phone rang and rang, but Dad didn't pick up.

I paced as far as I could, stretching out the curly phone cord,[1] listening to my landline phone ring until it switched to voice mail. "Come on, Dad!"

I rushed to the couch and punched the pillows a few times until I realized Dad wouldn't know or recognize our landline number. Like most people, he probably ignored all unknown callers.

And I couldn't tell him to switch from approving my cell phone to my landline number when I was completely cut off. I'd only memorized his home number, not his office.

I couldn't look up that office number, either. Not only had my mom left with my phone in her pocket, but even if she'd gone brunching without her laptop, she'd already changed the Wifi password.

I'd have to reach him some other way.

I searched through my pockets again and found a key scrap of paper. Dad had given me his wife's number too. Because Mom had already confiscated my phone yesterday, I'd written it down on paper. That meant I still had it.

I forced myself to call Mrs. Wong without agonizing about the awkwardness.

Ring, ring, ring. At least her voice recording sounded nice, so I left a message. "Hi, this is Edan Sze. I don't know if, uh, Edward told you, but I'm his daughter from before. I think he's in danger. Please call me back at this number, which is our landline. My mom took my phone and grounded me."

Okay, I officially sounded insane. Mrs. Wong would never call me back.

Step two. I called Barstow again. No answer.

At least Callie picked up. I told her right away, "I need help!"

"With what?" she panted.

"My dad! I think the killer will go after him next."

"But why?" She didn't stop running.

"We all think he was Mrs. L's lawyer, and he's keeping her secret out of client confidentiality, even after her death. But the killer won't know that. He'll go after my dad. I just found my dad, and I don't want to lose him!"

"Hold up." A horn screeched by. Callie's shoes continued to

smack against the pavement. "Okay. Let's say you're right. What do you want me to do about it?"

"Warn my dad!"

"And save Barstow at the same time? Argh!"

"You're a superhero."

She snorted. "Okay, give me your dad's number. I'll do my best to clone myself."

She really was a) the best and b) in an impossible position.[2] "Thanks. I'll try to call my mom and get her to change her mind. Then I can go to my dad!"

"Good luck with that."

Still, I hung up feeling a smidge more encouraged. At least I was doing something. I tried my mother next.

Forks rang against plates and people chattered while she said hi.

I told her right away, "Mom, I love you."

She sucked in her breath. "I love you too, Edan. Is that the emergency?"

"Listen, Mom, I think Edward might be in danger." I explained how he was a lawyer (which she knew), how Mr. Linkletter had said Mrs. L had met with Edward the night she died, and how I thought Mrs. L had consulted my dad as a lawyer, after hours. We knew the school had lost money and hired forensic accountants. My father wouldn't break confidentiality, but the killer wouldn't know that. "I've got to warn him, Mom. Please."

She sighed. "Are you sure?"

I knew what she was saying. *Are you sure this isn't a ploy to get out of being grounded? Are you sure you're not overreacting?* "Yes. So sure. Plus I'm worried about Barstow. He set a trap for whoever stole the money. A trap in his desk and in mine. And then he hung up on me!"

Now Mom sounded concerned. "Barstow set a trap for a thief at your school? With a killer out there? Who is it?"

"He wouldn't tell me. He hung up."

She swore under her breath. "I'll have to send Garrett out."

"No, please, Mom. Remember, I talked to the company that sells barrels in Las Vegas, and someone who looked like Garrett tried to buy one!"

She didn't answer. For a second, I thought she'd cut the call. "That doesn't make any sense, Edan."

"I asked who bought a 55 gallon drum, and he described a man with a broken nose and acne scars who sounded a *lot* like Garrett Smith."

"Coincidence," she said finally.

"Is it? Mom, he's always working out. He's strong enough to fit people in barrels. He can hike trails, no problem, and no one would ever suspect him because he's the police! *Please,* Mom."

She sighed. "I won't believe it. I can't. I know him better than anyone in the world except you."

"Please, Mom! If you're wrong and send him after Barstow—"

"I see your point," she said. "I can't put Barstow in danger. But if *you're* wrong and I *don't* send him after Barstow, I'd feel responsible if someone hurt your best friend."

"Call Barstow's parents. They're on his side."

"Me too," she said softly. "Okay. I'll call them. You sit tight and let me organize this. Then I'm coming home. Be there in a flash."

42

S tuck in the apartment, where it all began, I paced, pulled at my hair, and willed everyone to call me back.

This is my case. I'm supposed to run this![1]

Instead, I made myself drink water and eat an apple, in case I got stuck on a manhunt for hours. The way police do.

For a manhunt, I'd need to pack. I hit the bathroom and accidentally knocked over Mom's deodorant, but caught it by the pink cap before it fell in the toilet and set off Mr. Villalobos downstairs.

I opened the medicine cabinet by pulling the edge of the mirror toward me. I replaced the deodorant beside her fancy glass bottle of bath salts. Still, I couldn't rip my eyes away from the pink cap. It nagged me even as I shut the mirrored door.

A few minutes later, I set my glass on the table with a thunk. The table wobbled. The colour pink jabbed my memory again, and I jumped to my feet.

Pink. Pink like Mom's diary!

Trapped in the apartment, I could still locate Mom's journal. She might have written about last Friday night with her boyfriend.

Did Garrett have a true alibi? Or had he bought that 55 gallon drum we found at Red Rock, plus another one for Mr. L?

I checked behind the toaster, where Callie had found Mom's diary when we made the muffins. Nope, not a trace. I searched the cabinets, even grabbing a stepping stool so I could clamber up and run my hand along the top. Not here either, although a rectangle in the dust showed that she'd left it here not that long ago.

I searched the kitchen drawers next, the oven, the drawer under the oven with the roasting pan, the fridge, and the freezer. Don't laugh. I've found good stuff in the freezer before, including expensive chocolate.[2]

This time, I poked through the freezer shelves and found a bag that felt a little too thin and rectangular, labeled LIVER.

Dead giveaway. We hate liver.

I exhaled. "Thanks, Mom."

I rushed into the bathroom, locked the door, and ripped open my mother's diary.

I flipped to last Friday night. She'd written in code by making certain letters look like numbers. Easy to decode and figure out. For example, 50 r0mant1c was "so romantic."[3]

So romantic! Garrett was late again for dinner. He called at 9 p.m. and said he'd been held up. But he made it up to me by taking me for a midnight dinner, and we laughed until we fell asleep in each other's arms …

Barf. But she'd marked the times, sort of. A midnight dinner? He'd been *three hours* late?

Oh man. That gave him plenty of time to grab Mrs. Linkletter after she'd met with my dad.

For last Saturday, I read

Hard to wake up G, but we had the whole apartment to ourselves until the afternoon. Edan went to the climbing gym with her friends.

Mom must not have realized that the picture of us by the trail was from the Red Rock Canyon. Either she hadn't taken a good look at it, or maybe it hadn't even gone through properly. I'd check my phone when I got it back.

I did sometimes walk past a Red Rock Gym in our neighborhood. No wonder she thought I'd gone there instead of the Red Rock Canyon, a whole hour's round trip away.

It also explained why, if she'd mentioned we'd hit the climbing gym, instead of the canyon, Garrett hadn't bothered to stop snoring.

The guy slept like a mountain. A guilty conscience must not have gnawed him awake.

Monday
  Edan's history mark dropped. I asked to speak to Mr. Carver, but he hasn't answered my email.

I rolled my eyes. Who cared about that right now? Although worrying about history meant that Mom hadn't heard about Barrel Woman yet. Sure enough, her writing turned spiky in the next paragraph.

Impossible. They found a body in a barrel at Red Rock Canyon, and my own daughter and Callie were called to the station!

She must have brought her diary to work. I skimmed the next few paragraphs until I found another note about Garrett.

I left three messages asking Garrett to meet me at the station to help Edan. When he finally got back to me, he said he was on duty. It's so hard dating a police officer, especially in the middle of an investigation …

Garrett had gone AWOL on Monday. He'd told Mom he was working late, but what if he'd driven to Red Rock to try and hide the evidence?

43

While I quietly freaked out about Garrett, someone knocked on our apartment door.

Should I answer or not?

I thought of the Red Rock Killer and realized, *Not*. What the heck!

"Edan?" called a man's voice. A familiar voice, but not Garrett Smith's.

I frowned. My father? No, a higher male voice, more uncertain. One that reminded me of school.

"Edan, it's Mr. Carver. Are you there?'

Mr. Carver. My history teacher.[1]

I hunched between the sink and toilet as if my teacher had X-ray vision, although I could hardly cram myself into such a tiny space. My heart practically banged into my throat like it wanted me to swallow it.

"Edan, we need to talk."

Why couldn't he wait 'til Monday like a normal teacher? I waited, Mom's pink diary pressed against my stomach.

What if he forced his way in?

I glanced around the bathroom. No window, so I couldn't escape outside, even if I wanted to fall down two stories. I couldn't hide properly under the sink or behind the toilet. I *could* climb in the shower stall, but he might shoot me through it.

I needed a weapon. But what?

If only Mom hadn't taken my phone. What did people do in the olden days if they needed help and the phone was literally in the next room?

I reached behind the mirror medicine cabinet to claim Mom's one indulgence, the glass bottle of fancy bath salts that she used to soak her feet in the sink. I'd smash it on his head if he dared come in. I shelved the diary in its place. "I brought your article from the Civil War," Mr. Carver said, all casual-like, as if teachers regularly tried to break into students' homes.

I tucked myself between the sink and toilet again. Who needed to breathe at a time like this? Maybe he'd assume no one was home.

I hoped he couldn't break down the door or jimmy the lock. Hoped that Mom would blaze home and say, *Get away from my daughter.*

"You left it in your desk."

Left what?

As if reading my mind, he said, "The article that came in the mail. Very clever of you to send it to the classroom."

I tensed. Mr. Carver had come to our apartment for only one reason. He'd killed the Linkletters, and he thought I'd pinned it on him.

Barstow had mailed that page from an old Harpers Weekly Magazine with the sketches.

Mr. Carver had mistaken the article for me teasing him.

Why? Why would Mr. Carver have killed Mr. and Mrs. Linkletter?

No, I reminded myself, *Mrs.* and Mr. Linkletter. He killed our principal first.

What did I know about Mrs. Linkletter, besides the fact that she'd visited her grandkids in New Jersey, and that she sang out "Good morning, Foresters!" before turning over the morning announcements to the students?

Wait. That wasn't quite right. She'd also told us to stay away from gambling.

"Casinos kill," she told us once.

How did that fit with what I knew about Mr. Carver? I racked my brain for his quotes.

War is a lottery in which nations ought to risk nothing but small amounts.—Napoleon

Sometimes you have to risk life, in order to live, and gamble death, to sacrifice life.—Anthony Liccione

I'd focused on war and Napoleon before. Now I noticed the other words, like lottery. And gambling.

When I brought up the Civil War, Mr. Carver suggested gambling with toothpicks.

He argued with Mrs. Linkletter and Mr. Eisen about money.

Someone had embezzled money from the school.

Both Barstow and me had our money stolen from Mr. Carver's classroom.

That thief/murderer/gambler history teacher now stood outside my door.

"Quite an interesting gift," said Mr. Carver. "I like how the top picture shows three men gambling with a barrel in the foreground."

I covered my mouth with my free hand. The sketch showed the rifleman standing in front of wine cask, a bulging cylinder made out of wood and held together with metal hoops.

I'd concentrated on the men and on the gambling, not the cask.

But the other name for a cask is *barrel*.

Mr. Carver thought I'd taunted him all this time with a Civil War drawing of gambling and barrels.

He'd killed Mrs. L over gambling after stealing money from the school. Then he'd killed Mr. L to cover up the first murder.

Now Mr. Carver had come to shut up the loud kid who'd finally figured it all out.

44

Should I risk running out of the bathroom to call 911 on the landline?

I'd have to cross the hallway to get there. Mr. Carver could peer through the peephole on the other side of the door. He'd probably hear my footsteps tromping like elephants, like Mr. Villalobos says. Then Mr. Carver could shoot me through the door.

Before I could decide, a different man growled, "Who are you?"

I recognized that voice. Garrett Smith. I clutched the bath salts. Had Garrett plotted with Mr. Carver, or had Mom sent him to save me while she protected Barstow?

"Hello, my name is Warren Carver. I'm Edan's history teacher. How are you?" Mr. Carver spoke like he'd never met Garrett before, but it could be an act.

I glanced down at the bath salts. Could I brain two men with this bottle instead of one?

Probably not.

"Fine." Garrett didn't sound impressed. "What are you doing here?"

"Edan is falling behind in history. Her mother reached out to me."

Not true, I screamed inside my head. *I mean, yes, I got 70 percent on a pop quiz, and Mom did reach out to him, but right now he's here to kill me like the Linkletters!*

"I've got it on my phone. See?" Mr. Carver must be showing him Mom's email.

"Huh. Let me contact her." Silence. I imagined Garrett texting Mom with his meaty fingers. It took him five minutes to type anything. At this exact moment, I voted for him to take a year. Long enough for Mom to come home and tell Garrett she never invited this guy over to our apartment.

"Nice day," said Mr. Carver.

"Not as hot as it could be," Garrett agreed.

Argh! Talking about the weather with a murderer![1]

Garrett's tone shifted. "Okay, she says that Edan does have a history teacher named Mr. Carver. Let me send her your picture."

"What?"

Through our thin walls, I heard the shutter sound of Garrett snapping a photo with his phone. "You could be anyone saying you're Mr. Carver. She would've met you at parent-teacher meetings. Let's see if she gives you the okay."

She does not.

I practiced swinging my bath salts. I couldn't stay hidden and get a good arc unless I hid behind the bath curtain.[2]

"She says she never invited you here," said Garrett.

I sagged against the tile wall. *Thanks, Mom.*

"But if you want to come in and wait, she'll be home soon."

No, Mom!

"I've got a key. I can let you in."

No, Garrett!

Garrett inserted the key. He turned the bolt, and our apartment door creaked open.

45

I prayed. I'm not a religious person, but had very few options left. Like, almost zero.

Mr. Carver probably wouldn't try to break into the bathroom in front of Garrett. But what if he did? Or what if he didn't bother with the handle and shot me right through the wall?[1]

I lay down on my back on the wet floor of the shower stall,

bending my knees to place my feet on the floor. I balanced the bath salts on my stomach, where they heaved up and down with my breathing.

If Mom talked to my friends, they'd warn her. Right? Maybe brilliant Barstow had ID'd Mr. Carver. Maybe Barstow and Callie would bust in ahead of Mom.

Or the Linkletter kids would figure it out. Mr. Linkletter must've, since Mr. Carver killed him. The kids would avenge their parents.

Or the other cops would crack the case. That was their job.

In the meantime, I held the bath salts and let water droplets soak into my hair and into my clothes. *I don't want to die.*

"I don't see Edan," said Garrett. "You think she's expecting you? You called her first to set this up?"

"Oh, I bet she's expecting me. Smart girl, your Edan. Got a good head on her shoulders."

"She takes after her mother," said Garrett, not bothering to explain that I wasn't related to him.

"You seem pretty smart yourself. What kind of work do you do?"

"LVPD," Garrett said, and I liked the sound of that. Maybe the Las Vegas Police Department would intimidate my teacher into leaving.

"Tough job," said Mr. Carver. "In some ways, I believe it's not so different from my own work as a history teacher. You see people's histories playing out every day and every night. You could write a book."

What a strange thing to say. Garrett didn't answer.

Mr. Carver cracked his knuckles. I flinched, remembering him doing that when I opened the Civil War drawings. He must pop his knuckle when he got stressed, the way I rubbed my nose.

"Tell me again what you're doing here," said Garrett.

"Edan needs help," Mr. Carver said. I imagined his red eyebrows bouncing up and down like caterpillars.

"Enough help that you volunteered to tutor her on your own time on a Saturday?"

"I'm a giving kind of person," said Mr. Carver.[2]

"I get that," said Garrett. "Tell me more about you."

"Not much to tell. I read a lot. The kids make fun of me for writing a quote every day on the board, in chalk, but I think they look forward to it."

Not if you're a killer, buddy.

How could I warn Garrett without a phone? I could bang out SOS on the wall, but that would pinpoint my exact location for Mr. Carver. It would also infuriate Mr. Villalobos downstairs.

Wait! I wanted the police. For once, Mr. Villalobos's fury could work for me.

I flipped on my right side and tapped on the toilet base, near the floor, using the glass bottle of bath salts. Tap-tap-tap. Tap tap tap. Tap-tap-tap.

That spelled SOS in Morse code. Sort of. Too bad I couldn't make dash sounds on a toilet.

"You hear something?" Mr. Carver asked.

I tensed and paused with the bottle an inch away from the ceramic.

"I want to hear more about you," said Garrett. "I find it awfully strange that you'd show up outside our apartment. How'd you get in the building?"

"I used to live in this building. They kept the same default code to open the door."

Barstow and Callie used that code all the time, but I didn't remember Mr. Carver living here.

"Yeah? What's the code?" Garrett asked him.

"I'm not supposed to share it."

"But you're supposed to come in a building where you don't live any more? You work at Forester Middle School, don't you?"

"Sure do."

"For how many years?"

"Twelve years."

"You like that?"

For the first time, Mr. Carver paused. I wriggled in the bathroom. *Keep answering questions!*

Finally, Mr. Carver did. "I like the students. They're good kids, for the most part."

"But not your co-workers or supervisor?"

"I didn't say that."

"How'd you get along with Mrs. Linkletter?"

"All right."

"Just all right?"

"Some principals play favorites or give in to bullies. She didn't do that, and she she didn't interfere with my lesson plans."

"Did she interfere with something else?"

Suddenly, someone else banged on the apartment door, shocking all of us. "Edan, Edan, Edan!"

46

I almost yelled back in response, but Garrett's footsteps thundered into the hall. He threw open the door. "Barstow. What are you doing here?"

"I have to tell Edan about Mr. C—" Then, even from inside the bathroom, I heard Barstow suck in his breath. He must have spotted our teacher in the living room.

"Mr. Carver? What about Mr. Carver?" Garrett asked slowly.

"Nothing. I gotta go. Excuse me."

"Just a minute, Barstow—"

Barstow's feet rushed away. Callie's voice floated in from down the hall. "Barstow!"

I stifled a gasp. *Don't hurt my friends.*

I heard someone slam and lock our apartment door.

Garrett said, "Interesting."

Mr. Carver chuckled, but goosebumps prickled on my arms as my teacher's voice grew closer, advancing from the living room to the bathroom. "I wouldn't listen to those kids."

"No? Barstow always struck me as a very bright child."

"He's smart, no question about that. But good judgement? He and Callie and Edan get too riled up. Too much imagination."[1]

"I disagree. I'd better check with her mother to make sure Edan is all right."

Oh, crap. If Garrett stared at his phone, Mr. Carver might attack him and then me! I tapped on the toilet again, louder now. Tap-tap-tap. Tap tap tap. Tap-tap-tap.

"Where is Edan?" Mr. Carver raised his voice. "I want to chat with her. Help her out."

I hit the toilet as hard as I dared. The bottle reverberated in my hands.

Garrett said, "Barstow stared at your hands. What stained your fingers purple?"

I tensed. Barstow's theft detection dye. I already knew that Mr. Carver had taken the print from my desk. Those stains proved that Mr. Carver had searched our desks, and probably stolen from the school too.

Tap-tap-tap. Tap tap tap. Tap-tap-tap.

"There's that noise again," said Mr. Carver. He must have as good ears as Mr. Villalobos.

Better ears, maybe.

Tap-tap-tap. Tap tap tap. Tap-tap-tap.

"I'll go make sure everything's all right," said Mr. Carver.

"You sit down," Garrett growled.

"I'd rather not."

"You get one more chance. Sit down or I'll *make* you sit down," Garrett said.

"THAT'S IT! I've had enough of your banging and hollering," Mr. Villalobos called from his apartment downstairs. "I'm calling the cops RIGHT NOW!"[2]

<h1 style="text-align:center">47</h1>

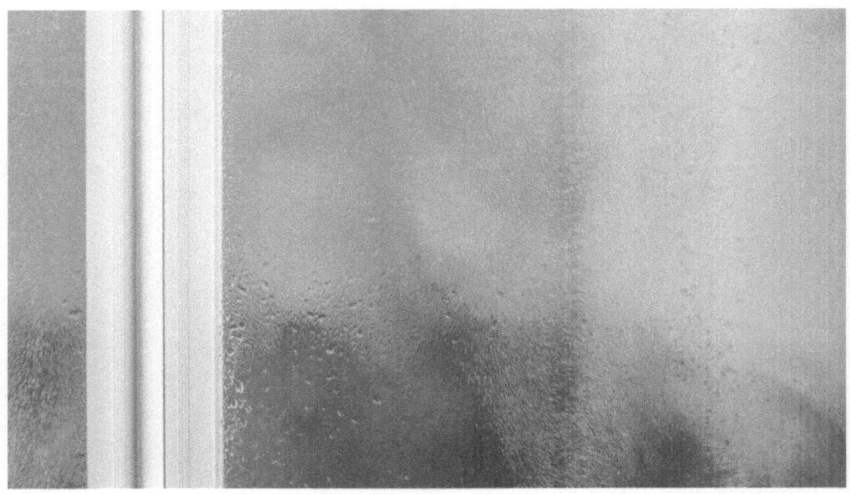

A small silence followed Mr. Villalobos's announcement. Quiet enough for me us to hear our neighbor giving the cops what for.

Mr. Carver said to Garrett, "Don't you dare pull a gun on me." He kept his voice calm.[1]

I squeezed my eyes shut and rolled onto my back on the shower floor, as flat as I could possibly get, clenching the bath salts with my right hand. *Don't let me die here.*

"I have reason to call you in for questioning," said Garrett. "You're a teacher at the school where the principal and her husband have been killed. I found you loitering outside our apartment—"

A bullet pinged through the hallway.

Don't die, Garrett!

Once my ears cleared, I heard Garrett calling for backup.

Good not dying, Garrett!

I huddled on the still-wet floor of the shower stall, damp but breathing and unbloodied, until someone hammered on our apartment door.

"POLICE!"

Come in! I wanted to scream, but I clung to my bath salts and held my breath until I finally heard them hauling Mr. Carver away.[2]

48

"You can come out now, Edan." Garrett knocked on the bathroom door.

I unsealed my lips and whispered, "Is he gone?"

"Goner than gone."

"You sure?"

"I promise."

"Okay." I tried to lever myself up, but my hands had cramped around the bath salts. It took a minute to let go of the bottle and to carefully push myself up from the slippery floor using both hands.

"Edan!" my mother hollered from down the hallway.

My heart sang. "Mom!"

Garrett spoke against the bathroom door. "Let's get you out safely, and you can talk to your mom and give a statement to the police."

I tiptoed toward the bathroom door, but before I unlocked it, I asked Garrett one last question. "Why'd you want a 55 gallon rain barrel?"

"How'd you know about that?" Garrett sighed through the wood. "You and your friends."

I waited.

"Your mom wanted a rain barrel for your birthday."

I clapped a hand over my mouth. I did ask for one, to conserve water, what felt like a million years ago.[1]

"She showed me a website where we could buy a fancy one for almost two hundred bucks. I figured I could buy one for cheap from the source and then stick a spigot on it,[2] but they wouldn't sell direct to the public."

"Wholesale only," I agreed, and unlocked the bathroom door.

Garrett's broken nose had never looked so beautiful in my life.[3]

49

Mom accompanied me to the police station. She wiped her eyes while I gave my statement to Officer Peters and Officer Evans.

Afterward, Mom held my hand very tight "I'm so sorry, honey. I never would have put you in danger. I had no idea what would happen to you without your phone!"

"You didn't know. Heck, Mr. Carver never exactly warned us."

"He figured out how smart you were," she said.

I shook my head. "Barstow knew and proved it by booby trapping his desk,[1] with Callie right behind him.[2] EBC did it. Could I please talk to them?"

"Of course." She rummaged in her purse for my phone. "Clever of you to use Mr. Villalobos as a 911 system, though."

"Thanks! I was desperate." I texted my friends.

EDAN

How did you know it was Mr. Carver?

CALLIE

Want to come over?

"Can I go to Callie's house?" I asked Mom.

Mom shook her head. "I don't want you out of my sight for the next week."

"Please, Mom. I'll ask if you can come too. I need to know what happened, and they want to see me."

"That makes sense," she allowed, and called Mrs. Yang from her own phone.

Twenty minutes later, Callie squeezed me extra tight with her muscle-y arms while Barstow grinned like a proud dad.

Then I dragged Barstow in for the hug too, which he endured for a whole two seconds.

"Couldn't have done it without you," I told them.

"I'll say," said Callie, drawing away and flipping her ponytail. "Barstow worked out that Mr. Carver was a gambler, and that's how he got in trouble with Mrs. L."

"From his quotes?" I asked Barstow. "I finally put that together while I was trapped in the bathroom."

Barstow nodded. "Yeah, but also the way he taught. He divided us into teams. We debated different positions, Axis vs

Allies, negotiating treaties, voting on who was more likely to win
... "

"Once you pointed that out, I realized that he sometimes even
bet on *us*. Remember the pizza party at Thanksgiving?" Callie
grinned before she caught herself.

"Yup." Our team had won. We all got pizza, but the winners
chose their slices first. "He could have planned that without a
gambling problem."

Barstow shook his head. "He bet on everything, like those
soldiers you said bet on their own fleas. Mrs. L's warnings about
gambling stepped up too, until the day she disappeared. I checked
Mr. Carver out. He was riddled with debt, even with a steady job."

"Well, teachers are underpaid," said Callie.

Barstow tilted his head. "Yeah, but most of them don't steal from
the school until the principal notices."

"So Mrs. Linkletter needed my dad's help after she caught Mr.
Carver?" I asked.

"She'd contacted forensic accountants and the school board too,"
said Barstow. "I found some of Mr. Carver's correspondence."

"Legally?" I asked, and Barstow held a finger to his lips.

Boy, that guy really knew everything.

"Aight," said Callie, imitating Barstow and his dad. "You're the
brilliant one."

Barstow shrugged. "I might not have thought of tapping on the
toilet like Edan."

"Genius," I agreed.

Callie laughed. "Well, maybe not genius, but definitely creative."

We all fist bumped each other.

"So we're going to be okay?" I asked them.

Barstow half-grinned. "'Course. And you can spend time with
your dad. I bet your mom will let you go to the BBQ now."

"Yep. She gave me my phone back too."

High fives all around for that one.

"Is it weird that we're not even 14 years old, and we've already nailed a killer?" I asked. "What else do we have to look forward to?"

Callie shrugged. "I still want to beat my record in the 100 Free."

Barstow grinned at her and then at me. "I downloaded two new mods on Terraria."

"I want to get to know my dad and his whole other family. Still. What're we going to do this summer?" I waggled my eyebrows at them. "We could get into a lot of trouble."

"Edan!" Mom walked over to us and ruffled my hair. "No trouble for you. Not if I can help it."

I kissed her cheek. I'd have to remember to put her diary back in the freezer before she figured out I'd moved it.

In the meantime, our summer spread before us, bright with promise.

———

If you enjoyed Red Rock, massive thanks for leaving a review online or telling a friend. You rock!

I hope Edan's adventures will continue. Please stay tuned to EBC through Kickstarter and my newsletter.

Did you know Edan has a cousin named Hope Sze who solves her first mystery in **Code Blues**?

Edan doesn't know Hope. But the two cousins will meet up one day in an incendiary combination.

EDAN'S BANANA MUFFINS
INSPIRED BY THE "BEST EVER BANANA MUFFINS" ON FOOD.COM

My friend Geneviève saved me from dry, overly heavy banana muffins with this.

Ingredients

- 3 large ripe bananas
- 3/4 cup sugar
- 1 egg. Beat it up a bit.
- 1/3 cup melted butter
- 1 teaspoon baking powder
- 1 teaspoon baking soda
- 1/2 teaspoon salt
- 1 1/2 cups flour

Optional: 1/2 to 3/4 cup chocolate chips

Directions

1. Mash those bananas up.

2. Add sugar and the mildly beaten egg.

3. Add melted butter.

4. Add the dry ingredients and bake in muffin tins at 375 degrees for 20 minutes.

ACKNOWLEDGMENTS

Hooray for my Kickstarter backers! Thank you for bringing Edan and Red Rock to life.

I would not have written this book without the International Thriller Writers. For their best first sentence contest, I wrote, seemingly from nowhere, "My mom told me I could do whatever I wanted the whole summer I turned fourteen, so I decided to find the Red Rock serial killer."

That won best first sentence from New York Times bestseller Allison Brennan. I sent her the opening to critique as my prize.

Then ITW offered a contest for a scholarship for a BIPOC middle grade crime novelist. I kept writing and submitted *The Red Rock Killer*. ITW awarded me the scholarship (!) and told me that R.L. Stine, one of the esteemed judges, wanted to meet and greet me (!!!!!).

Hot diggity!

I love the cover by Debbie at The Cover Collection.

Instagram's @dogtor.daisy generously drew Edan's interior art.

Margaret MacDonald and Dawn Kiddell monitor my spelling gremlins.

My ITW critique group checked Edan out, my children helped finesse the language (they don't say hot diggity), my husband keeps the home fires burning when I sail off to New York, and my dogs are the best because they are dogs. Thank you all.

ABOUT THE AUTHOR

Melissa Yi lives in Canada with three humans and two rescue dogs.

Sign up for Melissa's newsletter at www.melissayuaninnes.com *or directly at* https://melissayi.substack.com/

If you liked Edan, please let your friends know in person or online.

And rock on!

amazon.com/author/myi
facebook.com/MelissaYiYuanInnes
x.com/dr_sassy
bookbub.com/authors/melissa-yi
instagram.com/melissa.yuaninnes
pinterest.com/melissayi_

ALSO BY MELISSA YI

Hope Sze Medical Crime

Hope Sze novels Amazon series link: https://amzn.to/2GmIKUM

Flamingo Flamenco (Hope Sze short story)

No Air (Hope Sze radio drama)

Code Blues (Hope Sze 1)

Notorious D.O.C. (Hope Sze 2)

Family Medicine (essay & Hope Sze novella combining the short stories *Cain and Abel, Trouble and Strife, and Butcher's Hook,* which are also available separately)

Terminally Ill (Hope Sze 3)

Student Body (Hope Sze novella post-Terminally Ill; includes radio drama *No Air*)

Blood Diamonds (Hope Sze short story)

The Sin Eaters (Hope Sze short story)

Stockholm Syndrome (Hope Sze 4)

Human Remains (Hope Sze 5)

Blue Christmas (Hope Sze short story)

Death Flight (Hope Sze 6)

Graveyard Shift (Hope Sze 7)

Scorpion Scheme (Hope Sze 8)

White Lightning (Hope Sze 9)

Hope's Seven Deadly Sins Thrillers

The Shapes of Wrath (Hope Sins 1: Wrath)

Sugar & Vice (Hope Sins 2: Gluttony)

Killing Me Slothly (Hope Sins 3: Sloth) [Kickstarter anticipated Sept 2024]

MORE MYSTERY & ROMANCE NOVELS BY MELISSA YI

The Italian School for Assassins *(Octavia & Dario Killer School Mystery 1)*

The Goa Yoga School of Slayers *(Octavia & Dario Killer School Mystery 2)*

Wolf Ice

High School Hit List

The List

Dancing Through the Chaos

SCINTILLATING SPECULATIVE FICTION SERIES

Chinese Cinderella, Fairy Godfathers & Beastly Beauty

Dog vs. Aliens, Grandma Othello & Shaolin Monks in Space

Tiger Girls & Vulture Gods

UNFEELING DOCTOR SERIES (MELISSA YUAN-INNES)

The Most Unfeeling Doctor in the World and Other True Tales From the Emergency Room (Unfeeling Doctor #1)

The Unfeeling Doctor, Unplugged: More True Tales From Med School and Beyond (Unfeeling Doctor #2)

The Unfeeling Wannabe Surgeon: A Doctor's Medical School Memoir (Unfeeling Doctor #3)

The Unfeeling Thousandaire: How I Made $10,000 Indie Publishing and You Can, Too! (Unfeeling Doctor #4)

Buddhish: Exploring Buddhism in a Time of Grief: One Doctor's Story (Unfeeling Doctor #5)

The Unfeeling Doctor Betwixt Birthing Babies: Poems About Love, Loss, and More Love (Unfeeling Doctor #6)

The Knowledgeable Lion: Poems and Prose by the Unfeeling Doctor in Africa (Unfeeling Doctor #7)

Fifty Shades of Grey's Anatomy: The Unfeeling Doctor's Fresh Confessions from the Emergency Room (Unfeeling Doctor #8)

Broken Bones: New True Noir Essays From the Emergency Room by the Most Unfeeling Doctor in the World (Unfeeling Doctor #9)

THE EMERGENCY DOCTOR'S GUIDE SERIES (MELISSA YUAN-INNES)

The Emergency Doctor's Guide to a Pain-Free Back: Fast Tips and Exercises for Healing and Relief

The Emergency Doctor's Guide to Healing Dry Eyes

NOTES

CHAPTER 1

1. I sat at my keyboard, ready to enter the International Thriller Writers' Best First Sentence Contest. This line popped in my head almost verbatim. The only difference is one word: "My mom told me I could do whatever I wanted the whole summer I turned fourteen, so I decided to find the Red Rock **serial** killer."

   So many questions exploded in my mind. Why would a teenager go after a serial killer? How could she do it?

   Would her mother try to stop her?

   Where is Red Rock?

   I couldn't wait to find out.

   Sometimes lines just fall out of the sky. The poet Ruth Stone could occasionally "hear a poem coming toward her—hear it rushing across the landscape at her, like a galloping horse" (Elizabeth Gilbert, *Big Magic*).

   That's why this entire book feels like magic to me.

2. When I looked up Red Rock afterward, I found two hiking trails. First up, the Red Rock Canyon outside Las Vegas, once the bottom of the ocean floor, where you can now find dinosaur tracks petrified on rock peaks.

   The second Red Rock hit was in Quebec, the Canadian province where my main protagonist, Dr. Hope Sze, finds murderers and saves lives during her family medicine residency.

   I'd lived in Quebec during my own medical training and through Hope's adventures. Time for a change.

   Viva Las Vegas!

3. This is totally me. My parents used to drag us camping because my dad loved fishing. I wanted to stay home and read. At university, my classmates adored camping and invited me to hike frozen waterfalls. Why?

4. The name Edan leapt out at me, even though it dooms her to two names that will flummox readers. Just pretend it's spelled Eden Z.

5. Not a typo. The first time I heard this, a woman put on an accent and said, "Your money no good here!" It stuck in my head.

CHAPTER 2

1. Like Edan, I brace myself every time a stranger says my name. For her, remember, long Ē, short ă.

2. It took 12 years of advocacy to rename this street in honour of Martin Luther King, Jr.

3. All I wanted were the free snacks.

CHAPTER 3

1. The inside of the police station is, in my mind, somewhat combined with the much smaller station in North Glengarry, Ontario, since I didn't manage to visit this one in Vegas.
2. Author David F. Kruger queried about interviewing a minor without a parent present. Nevada police are allowed to do this. They don't need to ask consent. Depending on your state, though, a child's statement obtained this way may not be allowed in court.

CHAPTER 4

1. As a kid, I'd parrot what other people said, and it didn't bother me. If they said Barrel Woman, I'd say Barrel Woman.
2. I wish I had a summer of freedom. When I turned fourteen, I volunteered for the Red Cross.

CHAPTER 5

1. One nice thing about three best friends is that someone will usually play peacemaker.
2. This and Tina Fey's line about Photoshop are my take-home messages from *Bossypants*.
3. My children introduced me to Stardew Valley https://www.stardewvalley.net/. I find it relaxing.
4. I knew the victim and perpetrator within the first few pages. Author Marie Still suggested that Edan and friends might have noticed Mrs. Linkletter's absence, but as a kid, I went to class, administrators not on my radar. My daughter agrees.

CHAPTER 6

1. Youngsters, this is a reference the Jackson 5 song https://www.youtube.com/ watch?v=y2bVIBwpCTA. You're welcome.
2. Although we never meet Mrs. Linkletter, I feel like we know her.
3. Not everyone starts screaming and crying in a crisis. Some turn inward.

CHAPTER 7

1. I've humiliated myself like this a time or two.
2. I channelled our high school music room.
3. My children don't insult my messiness. They know I wouldn't tolerate it, and they're just as messy. Stresses my husband/their dad right out.

CHAPTER 8

1. The sheer joy in this video: https://www.youtube.com/watch?v=qn3AvGDOTqw
2. Las Vegas does allow you to wash your car at home if your hose has a positive shut-off valve. However, they recommend you use a car wash because the run off will be recycled through a sanitary sewer.

CHAPTER 9

1. Once a guy told me I shouldn't wear red and purple together. I couldn't understand why he thought he should police my clothes. Another woman and I explained that he had no sense of art or fashion.
2. Huge problem. It means that either artists either come from rich families or go into debt. I kind of want to see Edan's mom fulfill her acting dream now.

CHAPTER 10

1. I got feedback that a parent would never ground a kid for having a bike vandalized. I thought, but did not say, *You have not met my parents.*
2. The skull caverns are the most exciting part of Stardew Valley and the closes you can come to dying as you battle bats
3. My children, especially my son, are very polite and share their video game loot. A sign that we raised them right!

CHAPTER 11

1. Don't try this at home!
2. Nevada and Texas are the only states that have legalized "forensic hypnosis." This was a popular tool in the 1970s but the science doesn't back it up. So this is a story of kids fooling around with stuff they shouldn't. Dah dah dah DAH!

CHAPTER 12

1. True story. Gotta wonder where the sweat pants came from!
2. Also a true story
3. I like a lot of fail safes. So does Edan.

CHAPTER 13

1. Places are usually too hot or too cold. Am I right? :)
2. As someone who's worn out her voice at work, I feel for Officer Peters
3. This is me. Once my friend asked me to come to a car show, and I explained that it would be like going to a blender show for me. Horrifying to him.
4. Often we get dismissed as too emotional or overreacting, even as adults. Especially women and people of colour.

CHAPTER 14

1. This was my basement as a kid
2. People talk about a "tell" during poker. I'm sure I have a dozen.

CHAPTER 15

1. "Hypnagogic cognition" or hypnagogia. Aristotle, Edgar Allan Poe, and Thomas Edison all referred to it in their creative process: https://serendipstudio.org/exchange/fquadri/hypnagogia-who-needs-lsd-when-you-can-just-sleep
2. Love dogs. Gotta include one, even only in Edan's mind.

CHAPTER 16

1. A school in Sherbrooke, Quebec, Canada invited a new hypnotist to do a show and five girls seemed unable to emerge from the effects of "mass hypnosis." He called his mentor for help. One girl was stuck for five hours! https://www.cbc.ca/news/canada/montreal/2nd-hypnotist-rescues-students-stuck-in-trance-1.1240499#:
2. Different states have different rules, but these are the regulations in Nevada.
3. I didn't carry any money as a kid, but I kept an emergency $20 in medical school.

CHAPTER 17

1. I worry about money like this, but actually Edan has a more healthy attitude than I did at that age, probably because she has Callie and Barstow.
2. I feel for Barstow. How can he protect himself from any police attention and still contribute equally to the investigation?

CHAPTER 18

1. It's no fun to be poorer than everyone else.
2. I've totally been Barstow, trying to help with information, sometimes hurting people's feelings with my bluntness. Now I try to think and rephrase in a more tactful way.

CHAPTER 19

1. Yup. After too many shocks, you shut down.
2. Barstow's such a good guy.

CHAPTER 20

1. My keyboards do suffer from my eating habits.
2. They still have pay phones in Vegas! I found a website listing.

CHAPTER 21

1. The contrast in emotion makes me laugh. I'm emotional like Callie, and my husband is low key like Barstow.
2. Now that I've stepped a toe in the acting world, I can tell you that it's unpaid and underpaid, especially at the beginning. If you want more of a guarantee, combine it with other skill sets like lightning, sound, or directing.

CHAPTER 22

1. One feedback that I remember from my swimming lessons.
2. The police pay a key role in real life, and I want to pay homage to that in my books too.

CHAPTER 23

1. My friend Geneviève makes the best banana muffins. Recipe enclosed at the end.
2. I love how the kids know stuff like fire hazards. Our family does end up stacking stuff on the counter, but not quite behind the toaster oven.

CHAPTER 24

1. My family and I would do something like this.
2. I'm sorry for the brutality of this.

CHAPTER 25

1. I know this woman. Part of me is this woman, as well as Edan.
2. I'm happy to use the "all Asians look alike" bias for Edan's benefit.

CHAPTER 26

1. Drives me wild when fictional amateur detectives believe they've cracked the case without evidence.
2. A possibility beyond devastating.

CHAPTER 27

1. I'm pretty proud of this slogan.
2. So hard to try and break this to your mom.

CHAPTER 28

1. The helplessness of not being able to control the grown ups around you.
2. As did we, until very recently.

CHAPTER 29

1. This company does exist, by the way.
2. The technology is there. Someday I might spoof my own family.

CHAPTER 30

1. I think this happened to me. Maybe more than once.
2. Thrilled to include the actual sketches, which have now entered the public domain.

CHAPTER 31

1. It's extra shocking when you know someone, and the hits keep coming.
2. Plus when I was in Las Vegas, at least once, one bus didn't come at all. I waited about ten minutes before and after.

CHAPTER 32

1. I used to have an ugly yellow shirt for gym.
2. Questions. Uncertainty. Only her friends make it easier for her.

CHAPTER 33

1. You know what I'm talking 'bout https://www.youtube.com/watch?v=yCOPJi0Urq4
2. Gotta love kids who can handle grown ups. It's a skill.

CHAPTER 34

1. Have you ever detected your own features on someone else? Delight, dismay ... depends on your relationship.
2. Sometimes it's easier when you're little.
3. My husband used to play WoW in a guild called "Blood, Bath, and Beyond."
4. Yes. I joined TikTok for BookTok, but the dances were too fun. @myibooks if you want to find me!

CHAPTER 35

1. Over, under, through!
2. Originally, I called her Caro, which is a common nickname for Caroline for francophones, but less likely in Las Vegas.

CHAPTER 36

1. Doctors have to report certain things, like let the government know if someone is unsafe to drive, but lawyers are supposed to keep your information confidential.
2. Gut sense. Not infallible, but you know it when you feel it. As an adult, I tend to go by "trust but verify."

CHAPTER 37

1. As a mom, I would blow up too.
2. I was like this as a kid. *Sorry, and now I can go, right?*

CHAPTER 38

1. This is what strikes me about police officers in action. Movies focus on renegade cops, but real police tend to work together and follow the rules. You're less likely to convict someone otherwise.
2. Yes. I don't think people realize how much of police work is talking to people, trying to convince them to come in for help at the hospital, for example.

CHAPTER 39

1. My kids learned a surprising amount of pop culture history from YouTube, as well as general knowledge. My three-year-old son surprised me with "Flowers first bloomed during the Cretaceous period."
2. I don't know why they have a Green Valley in the desert. Las Vegas means "the meadows" because it was originally an oasis and a holy place to indigenous people, but the settlers have pumped it dry.

CHAPTER 40

1. This must seem so old school and sloth-like if you've never had to do it before.
2. Mom's setting boundaries and will assuage her guilt with a muffin. Ask me how I know.

CHAPTER 41

1. That's right, kids, you used to be tethered to your phone. Literally.
2. Go, Callie, go!

CHAPTER 42

1. The frustration when you're the hero(ine), but you're grounded #kidproblems
2. Other moms have given me this trick of where to hide yummy food, but I'm too impatient to wait for the chocolate to warm up after I liberate it.
3. Weak code, I know.

CHAPTER 43

1. The unbearable strangeness of your teacher showing up at your apartment.

CHAPTER 44

1. I could totally see my parents doing this.
2. When you're literally in a corner, bath salts seem like a good weapon.

CHAPTER 45

1. Guns are terrifying. If this is too scary, skip to chapter 48.
2. That's when you know this person is odd *and* a murderer.

CHAPTER 46

1. Too many problem-solving skills.
2. You know when one of the bad guys becomes one of the good guys?

CHAPTER 47

1. Yikes. The last thing Edan needs is to get caught between two guns.
2. Phew!

CHAPTER 48

1. I love how Edan tries to help the desert on her birthday.
2. This is what my family would do.
3. Amazing how good people look once they help save your life.

CHAPTER 49

1. Love this. Seems like a Bobbsey Twins thing to do.
2. We need Callie's speed and brains too.